Widows
and
Orphans

John Wesley Edwards

ISBN 978-1-64258-362-5 (paperback)
ISBN 978-1-64258-363-2 (digital)

Christian Faith Publishing, Inc.
832 Park Avenue
Meadville, PA 16335
www.christianfaithpublishing.com

PUBLISHER'S NOTE
This is a work of fiction. Names, characters, places, and incidents either are a product of the author's imagination or are used fictitiously, and any resemblance to actual persons, living or dead, events, or locales is entirely coincidental.

Printed in the United States of America

For Deborah

"I always told God, I'm going to hold steady on you, and you've got to see me through."
—Harriet Tubman

-FRIDAY-

*I*t is a matter of great concern to me that the recent events of my young life, about which many people are understandably curious, get put down on paper accurately. I'm the person these things happened to, and I'm the most qualified, if not the most talented, to write what I know to be the truth. I've given the subject of my life much careful thought, and I've arrived at the conclusion that as people learn from my humble example, they will be inspired to break away from their humdrum existence, spruce up their drab lives, and attain a new appreciation of me. Most of what follows really happened.

My story has humble though raucous political beginnings. Let me say that it doesn't matter to me who wins the next presidential election. I am trying to be neutral, but it does appear to me that Kennedy has the prettiest wife. Mom and Grandma and I have a Zenith TV, and we often see Kennedy and Nixon on the news. Nixon sort of fades into the background, his pallid face and drab gray suits blending together till the impression is that he's not there. Kennedy, on the other hand, looks like a healthy, rugged athlete, and his wife is stunningly beautiful, though she doesn't have a nice overbite like Dinah Shore. Maybe it's the fact that black and white TV isn't as good to Nixon as it is to Kennedy. Also Nixon sweats too much, and I don't trust perspiring people unless they're in the laboring class, but there you have Nixon with that pencil—thin streak of perspiration habitually perched upon his upper lip. I always wondered about that, what backbreaking work was he doing that made him sweat bullets?

At school I avoided politics because it gets some people very angry. In fact, I have traced the beginning of my story to a class discussion which had political implications, which led to a very personal resolution, which in turn led to a series of unforgettable events.

My school reminded me of one of the schools that Francie and Neeley attended in Brooklyn. Teachers, I reasoned, determined the character and quality of a school, and to a man of my artistic sensibilities, the teachers I had were unusually troublesome and perplexing and rough around the edges. And right here at the beginning, it's important to point out that I divide my life into a handful of categories, for I am nothing, if not highly and efficiently organized.

School, the closest thing I know of to actual captivity on Devil's Island, was one category; church was an alternate space-time dimension like the Twilight Zone; home was a safe haven from the strife of life. That made three categories. There was another division that consumed and defined me, but more on that later.

It's a good thing I know who I am or school would have squashed the life out of me a long time ago. School was an unhealed wound, and to my astonishment, the officials there had tagged me as difficult. I know this was a fact because Teacher told me so right to my face.

It happened like this. One day in class after I had offered an intelligent, blistering statement about the necessity of arming American school children with concealed weapons against a possible attack by the dirty Russian Commies, I couldn't help but notice that Teacher was slowly swinging her head back and forth and all the while she kept frowning disapprovingly at me.

"Just imagine our playground invaded," I implored. "Our lunchroom would be ransacked, and our athletic equipment room plundered. But if we were armed, we could use our desks as a barrier and mow those storm troopers down. It'd be like a turkey shoot."

Teacher pointed to the door at the rear of the room. I knew the routine. She joined me a few minutes later. I was sitting on the bench outside the door. I had nearly indented the wood with my backside. It was a very familiar place to me.

Teacher slapped her hands on her hips and glared at me. "Crosby," she said sternly, "your words and behavior dismay me. You are a very difficult child!"

I rest my case: I had been labeled.

I don't mean to give the impression that I hated teachers, because I didn't. Of course on the other hand, I didn't exactly want them to win the Irish sweepstakes either. Call what we had an uneasy truce. Besides, I don't think of myself as difficult. I think I'm full of amazing ideas, novelties, inspirations, innovations, and alternatives. But the label bestowed on me never went away.

Even the school principal got into the act once. On that occasion, she entered our classroom and came to the front of the room. She was a tall bulky woman who smelled like cigarettes. She breathed raspily and always wore brown clothing, including her socks. She had a scar running down her right cheek, and she never wore makeup. One of my classmates once referred to her as Blackbeard the pirate, a comment which got him into real trouble because he said it to the principal's niece who promptly reported the whole incident to her aunt.

The principal said she was there that day to observe our class and that we should enjoy the literature lesson. She told us to act normally and forget that she was even there. Then she parked herself in the back of the class and began observing. However, it was difficult to forget she was back there, what with her heavy raspy breathing behind us, competing with the sound of Teacher's voice up front. We all had to lean forward a little to hear today's lesson.

At one point, I raised my hand and politely asked if I could go to the restroom, which wasn't exactly what I wanted to do.

"Of course, Crosby," Teacher said pleasantly. "Hurry back now. We're about to begin a delightful reading adventure." We were all being elaborately polite today, all right.

I picked up my crutches and left the room. In the bathroom, all I did was wash my hands and then quickly returned to the classroom door in record time. I peeked inside. The principal had her head down, reading a paper in front of her. I slipped into the room very quietly and was behind her before she could see me. I kept moving up the aisle to my desk. But I had seen enough. The paper in front of the principal had my name on it. Now I knew who the principal was really observing.

The reading adventure was a story about twins named Larry and Mary, who helped people around their neighborhood. The twins called themselves the Sunshine Squadron. They managed, by their good works and perky personalities and positive attitudes, to transform a grumpy old man into a really unselfish, kindly gentleman, who afterwards fixed broken toys free of charge for all the boys and girls in the neighborhood. Later the Sunshine Squadron helped change two grouchy old ladies into sweet, grandmotherly, cookie-baking, generous types. It seemed the old man and the old ladies had simply been misunderstood for years and years, and that all they ever really needed for them to see the error of their ways and make a complete recovery was the kindness and acceptance of people like Larry and Mary. The twins accomplished all this in three days. I wanted to scream and nearly did.

Teacher closed the book and smiled at the class. "Now then, boys and girls, wasn't that a lovely story? Wouldn't you like to form your very own Sunshine Squadron someday?"

I raised my hand. Teacher glanced quickly at the principal in the back of the room and then gave me a searching look. "Yes, Crosby," she said guardedly.

As was my habit, I stood up to answer. I placed one hand on my desk for balance. "Where's part 2 of this story?" I asked reasonably. "You know, where reality sets in? Because life isn't like this. Did Larry and Mary go into the houses of these people? That wouldn't be a very smart move on their part, because terrible things happen when people lock their doors. What if the old man had taken them hostage and demanded a hefty ransom payment? Or what if the two old ladies had slipped them a Mickey Finn and turned them into zombies? Larry and Mary need to read their daily newspaper, because people sometimes do awful things." My voice rose a little. "And what about Larry and Mary? What if that whole Sunshine Squadron was a clever hoax, and the twins were actually members of the Nazi Party?

Sunshine Squadron—get it? The SS. And then once Larry and Mary got inside those homes, they could help themselves to some jewelry and some antiques and look for the secret rooms where the Jews were being hid."

Up front, Teacher's mouth had dropped open. She looked as if she might speak, but I plunged ahead.

"My point is that Larry and Mary don't resonate. I don't know anybody like them in real life. There has to be conflict or there is no story. This writer forgot basic story-telling techniques. The story would be better if it was about Larry, Curly, and Moe on the Sunshine Squadron. As it is now—Larry and Mary's story should have been printed on bathroom tissue because then at least it could have been put to a practical use."

I sat down abruptly. Teacher was a study in facial expressions. She glared and grimaced and glowered at me—and that was just when I was speaking. Now that I was seated, she looked madder than a hornet. She tried to speak and then stopped. Finally, she sputtered several disconnected statements. "It's a very sweet story! You have a morbid imagination! Take them hostage, you say? Members of the Nazi Party?"

There was more in the same vein. The upshot of all this was not surprising: I was sent outside to sit down on the bench I had come to think of as my own personal property.

And there I sat, thinking about a few stories I knew. Nothing was sunshiny about them. I thought about Dov Landau in the Warsaw Ghetto, and Reverend Jim Casey with the Joad family, and Francie and Neeley Nolan in Brooklyn, and Jody Baxter and his friend Fodderwing in Florida, and Anne Frank in Amsterdam.

Twenty minutes later, the bell rang, and the classroom emptied out. No one looked at me. I sat quietly for a moment and then scooted to the end of the bench near the classroom door. Apparently, Teacher and the principal had forgotten I was still outside. I could easily hear them talking.

"Let me just tell you how sorry I am," Teacher was saying. "I can't control what Crosby says. He is precocious and unpredictable. He told me he's reading the dictionary."

The principal's voice rasped out. "The dictionary? Surely he's pulling your leg."

"He's up to the Rs now," Teacher said bleakly. "He knows more words than I do. He is very crafty and erratic, and he has an opinion on everything."

"You don't owe me any apologies," the principal cut in. "We have a complete file on Mr. Crosby Hoggard in the office. He is an *enfant terrible*, a troublemaker, and a nuisance." She paused and sighed deeply. And then to my amazement, her voice suddenly became sympathetic and understanding. "We all know about the terrible tragedy that happened to him and his family a while back..."

I grabbed my crutches and lurched away toward the playground. People don't know me or understand me, and I don't need to listen to the past when it's brought up, because if you don't discuss the past, you can mostly make it go away and stay away. Right then I needed my stories and all the characters I loved and believed in. I wanted them to fill my head and keep me company. The past was no companion of mine.

That was the first time I had been observed by the principal. I didn't let it get to me. If somebody wanted to keep a file on me, that was their business. I was adjusting to the weird circumstances of my academic life in the only way I knew how: be prepared by reading ahead in the textbook, listen closely in class and respond accordingly.

And in keeping with that habit, one day recently in geography class, I was more than ready for that day's lesson. And when Teacher brought up uniformitarianism—the belief that all geological processes are the same now as they have always been—I immediately raised my hand.

Teacher more or less stared at me, her expression held something like pity and an old skepticism. "Yes, Crosby," she said warily. "What is it?"

I stood up. "You have ignored the unparalleled geological event known as Noah's flood," I said firmly. "Talk about interrupting the process." I thumped my hand on my textbook. "There can be no validity to what this book says if it ignores such a well-attested truth."

I sat down and watched Teacher. My classmates, such as they were, remained stonily silent.

Teacher frowned and said quietly, "We've been over this before, Crosby. This is not a class about religion, and you don't have a corner on the truth. This class is about world geography. There are many students here today who don't happen to believe there ever was a man called Noah and far less do they believe in a worldwide flood, as you have reminded us of so many times." Teacher's face changed a little. She softened her tone and said evenly, "Crosby, I respect your beliefs, but this is a school, not a church. We don't have time for discussions like this every day."

Teacher dropped the subject now and told the class to put their books away because the bell was about to ring. I was thinking about how satisfying it was to be labeled difficult. I couldn't help it if I was right. A man has to speak up when he has helpful information. I was also wondering if this incident would be duly reported, typed up, and stored permanently in the Crosby Hoggard file in the principal's office.

Lunch followed geography. When the bell rang that day, I grabbed my crutches and headed for the cafeteria. On the way there, Maria Lopez caught up to me and said hello. We had something in common: her father and mine used to drink together at Velma's Bar and Grille in the hills above Monte Vista. I think Maria made too much of that connection, as though she was now supposed to watch out for me. For a girl, she wasn't that annoying, but I didn't really feel I needed her help that much.

Maria was a quiet person, and I was careful and unambiguous with what I said when I was around her, but on the other hand, she could sometimes say the most confusing things to me.

Like the time when I fell on my face out on the playground because of a shove from behind by a boy named Clyde Winston. When Maria helped me up, I said it was all my fault and made a joke about being a stupid klutz and then quipped that at least I'd had a nice trip, but inside I was fuming. Maria told me I was too hard on myself, and when I tried to answer her, she hushed me and said, "You don't have to be clever all the time."

There's just no understanding some people. As for Clyde Winston, who, given the opportunity, would stomp on his own grandmother for a candy bar, his day was coming, all right. Besides, I felt fortunate that Clyde only shoved me down. Some days he knocked me down and then sat on me.

In the cafeteria, Maria always carried my tray and then, by a certain unspoken understanding, sat—not next to me—but relatively close by. We heard the usual comments on the way to our table: "Here comes the spic and the crip," and "See you next fall, Cros boy."

I've heard it all, and I've learned that ignoring gibes makes them go away for the most part. The source of almost all of the ridicule was Clyde Winston. He always had something to razz me about. He wasn't very creative, though. In fact, he was profoundly tiresome in his insults. He was overweight and had yellow teeth and stringy hair. His head was huge, and he wore glasses with Coke-bottle-thick lenses, which were always greasy. He looked like he regularly stood over a boiling vat of oil so it could splatter his glasses. He was more or less easy to ignore, being so predictable in his behavior. A shove here and an insult there from him were part of my daily routine.

When I was done with lunch, Maria again took my tray. She seldom went with me to the playground. It wasn't as though we were boyfriend and girlfriend.

I usually sat on a playground bench by myself and watched other students. I especially liked watching dodgeball and tetherball. I am a good spectator.

That day was one of the times when Maria remained close by. I wanted to say something to her about our fathers, something like: my father is dead and yours is alive. And that intersection of our father's drinking together at Velma's didn't form a connection between us. I needed to convince her that she didn't owe me anything, for then I could spare her a false sense of obligation. But right then it seemed wise not to stir things up. I saved all that for the classroom where the targets were clearly defined: teachers and textbooks.

Yet, even though Maria and I were not boyfriend and girlfriend, she was the subject of hours of my thought life. I knew about lust because the pastor of my church had preached about it quite frequently. I was hearing more about the wrong use of sex than the right use, which seemed to be the way God intended it. In fact, the right use and purpose was a little vague—it was given a grudging acknowledgement from time to time, but the wrong use was an elaborate array of wicked practices, which could only be referred to with red-faced, pulpit-pounding denunciations.

None of that applied to Maria. She was a good friend, and I couldn't make my thoughts mold her into what pastor called a vile woman, the subject of many of his sermons. I always wondered, though, why he didn't preach against vile men. The lesson from the pulpit was that women were more inherently evil than men. And I sure never raised my hand in church when I had a question, like I did in school. Pastor had a forbidding manner and always thundered sermons from the pulpit. He never addressed the congregation, he dressed us down. He usually concluded his sermons by telling us that God loved us in a technical distant manner. It was just that we needed a good old-fashioned fiery balling out on a regular basis to keep us in line.

Even though Maria sometimes occupied my thoughts, I didn't feel overpowered by her. She was kind and helpful and didn't call me names or remind me of things I didn't want to be reminded of. She had a certain pleasantness that I thought was attractive. And you could say she was pretty—even lovely—though in a different style than my mother and her sisters. My aunts were generally blond and blue-eyed and churchgoers and fascinating storytellers.

On the other hand, Maria was olive—skinned with clear brown eyes and smooth black hair. She was very shy, except around me, and a couple of times at school, we even had conversations that lasted a minute or two.

Church, by which I mean the building and the people it housed, was another major category in my life. Thankfully, church confined itself to Sundays only. I didn't know if I could take it much more than that.

Church services were loud but generally bearable. I always sat in the pews on the left side of the center aisle. I don't think it was my imagination, but it seemed to me that most young boys sat happily in those pews, where the church organ, and more importantly, where the church organist was situated up front on the platform. She was the pastor's wife, and she played a prosaic selection of hymns. However, she always slipped off her shoes to play the organ's floor pedals. It was quite a sight, those small, delicate, nylon-encased feet gently tapping out bass notes. Those of us on the left enjoyed faster-paced rhythms, for as the organist's dainty feet flew like little birds across the pedals, we would sing loudly and lustily unto the Lord.

I had once been to another church. It was when I had to attend a funeral a few years ago. The minister up front was wearing a long black robe. He looked so much like Zorro that I thought he was going to draw a sword and start carving zees any moment. After the funeral, when I told Mom about Zorro in the black robe, she said I should hush and respect other people's religious traditions. I did quiet down, but it was good for the imagination to have something diverting, like Zorro in the pulpit, to help you through a long funeral service.

Since I was more or less born and raised in a pew, I had over a period of time discovered many techniques to make church something I could live with. A pretty organist was a help. But the best way to pass the time was to go over plots and themes and characters from the novels I read. To me, church was basically a countdown to the benediction.

What sweeter day is there than Sunday? And leaving church on a sun-drenched California Sunday afternoon is what heaven must be like. The pungent scents of the resins from eucalyptus and oak and pepper trees hit you the second you stepped outside. The foothills stared you in the face. Just over the oak and madrone-studded hills was the Pacific Ocean. I lived on this side of the long gentle green-sloped ridge of the foothills, and I knew there was an ocean beyond. But the hills beckoned me. I stared at them too often. There was a secret in the hills that I wanted to understand. And it was only the hills, however, that I cared about. I was terrified of the ocean beyond, with its dark forbidding stormy black waters. At least that was how it looked on TV in the opening scenes of *Victory at Sea*. Even if my legs and feet worked right, and I could pass the physical, I would never want to join the Navy and go to sea.

16

So whenever I got out of church, I would halt briefly on the front stairs and breathe deeply of the aromas surrounding me, feeling blessed and renewed. Then I'd descend the steps and head around the corner for Orange Avenue and home.

Home was with my mother and grandmother, both widows. I'm the man of the house, and I am treated well. My clothes are always clean and freshly ironed. Grandma Plunk, my mother's mother, is the fastest woman with an iron in three counties. She hefted an iron like a gunslinger hefted his revolver. When I was younger, my favorite place was under the ironing board while she was ironing sheets. It was like a tent that smelled hot and steamy and comforting. She constantly warned me to be careful and not get in her way, but I crawled into my white tent whenever I could get away with it.

Of course now that I'm older, I don't crawl under there anymore; instead I simply pulled a chair near her when she was busy at the ironing board. Then I'd study or read, keeping two things near me—ironing smells and book smells, two very comforting aromas.

Neither my mother nor my grandmother knew exactly why I read like I did. Whenever they asked me, I'd always say it was a hobby, but my reading was my other world—more real than school, church, or home. I loved my novels and the characters in them more than I loved most of the people I knew. As a churchgoer, I figured that God would understand that he was the one who gave me books along with His Son, and that there'd be time for the people around me later. Right now, though, I fellowshipped constantly and happily with the Nolans and the Joads and the Baxters and the Ben Canaans and the O' Haras, and the Franks, to name a few.

And it seemed to me that books gave me more wisdom to live by than the church could offer. The wisdom I got in the church building consisted mostly of knowing how to avoid vile women and the devil. But I regularly went to another building that provided a different display of edification—the local library.

By comparison, the library was quieter than church. I felt free in the library, surrounded by all those ideas stuffed between book covers. Church took up offerings, but no librarian passed a plate, and most importantly, I didn't have to shake hands with anyone at the library. Church was an endless, unrelenting round of hand shaking, both going in and going out. Teacher said once that the ancient Romans shook hands as a custom so they could check for hidden knives on each other. For several weeks afterward, I graciously assured all the brothers and sisters at church who wanted to shake my hand that I wasn't carrying any concealed weapons, and that there was no need to grasp hands. But it didn't do any good. They just smiled and thrust out their hands anyway.

The problem with all those outthrust hands was that hands have palms—hot sweaty, germy, dirty palms. So on Sundays, I went home from church and used Ajax to wash my hands followed by a refreshing bleach rinse that made my eyes water. I often wondered why we couldn't institute a new church custom to replace the shaking of hands. Like winking knowingly at each other or bumping hips or yodeling a short tune.

Aside from the hand-shaking craze at church, I generally lived at peace there. I figured that both church and library had their respective advantages and benefits. Therefore, I lived with a certain equilibrium with both institutions.

So it was school and church and home and books that made up my life, which, within those categories—with all their ups and downs and times and seasons—I always knew that the books were most prominent.

A typical week for me had a more or less set routine: five days of school vexation, followed by weekend emancipation. Saturdays were serene, and Sundays were all about church. Mondays were inexorable, always mewling maniacally in the distance, waiting offstage to stomp me to smithereens. My problems, which were always fully developed and unanswerable, lifted and disappeared on weekends. Then came Monday with a fresh onslaught of aggravations in the classroom. There was no contest when it came to a comparison of my school week with weekends—school tended to be bleak and uninspiring, while Saturday and Sunday overflowed with blissful liberation. School was always trying to give me the Treatment, but I had learned how to cope—you got up on schooldays, dressed and walked down Orange Avenue to McClellan Road, crossed the street and entered the grounds of Andrew Johnson Junior High School. Then you went to class and waited for Friday.

And what were my problems that lifted on the weekends? Just the average issues plaguing any seventh grader. I thought about death and violence and the horror of the ovens at Auschwitz and how little children die without pity. I worried about people who were lonely and abused and wounded and hopeless and unloved and how I couldn't help them. I thought about being confined in a debtor's prison because Mom and Grandma and I couldn't make our rent payments on time. And sometimes the thought of being fatherless invaded my mind against my will, but that particular subject I always immediately and vehemently ignored and rejected. So really, I just had the usual, average, unanswerable problems that any twelve-year-old would have.

I prayed about these things on occasion, but the heavens were usually brass, and my faith was always weak to nonexistent. Still I held out the dim hope that God could do something amazing with my life if I just tried harder to be righteous and perfect and without sin.

And thus, my weekly routine sat ponderously in place, and I remained unshakable and more or less content under the circumstances.

However, one Friday in June, my typical school week was turned upside down by a portentious event which occurred during a social studies class. I didn't know it at the time, but what seemed blandly typical turned out to be extraordinarily exceptional. What happened on that day changed me forever. On that occasion, I went over a line I didn't usually cross.

The class was supposed to be discussing this year's election. Actually, Teacher was trying to get us into a discussion, but Fridays just don't lend themselves to politics when a glorious spring week-end was staring at you through the classroom window. The class sat there, apathetic and listless and waiting for the bell to ring. I could see Maria a few rows away from me. I liked her dark hair, which she usually wore brushed straight down with a curl at the bottom or sometimes tied back with a ribbon.

Teacher was still trying to get things moving and apparently to do so, she called on me, even though my hand was not up. "Crosby," she said lightly, with a tinge of false charm, "lately you've been very vocal in your negative views regarding Mr. Nixon. Why is that?"

I stood up. "I like his dog, Checkers, but he's no Eisenhower, that's for sure." I sat back down. I wasn't going to be manipulated into a discussion I didn't want to have.

Teacher grinned. "The last thing we need is another Eisenhower, Crosby. Look at the country's economy, for Pete's sake. Ike was an eight-year disaster."

I grinned back and kept my seat. I was hoping I could make one comment and then she'd cool her heels. I said, "If it wasn't for Ike, we'd all be heiling Hitler every morning instead of saluting our flag. I agree with all my relatives. Ike got the job done on D – Day and rescued Europe from an insane fascist future and wiped out all those Nazi thugs who wouldn't stop trying to destroy every Jew on the continent."

Teacher said we were supposed to be discussing the next election and not rehashing details about World War II or Jews. "You bring up irrelevant side issues," she said rather smugly. "Ike isn't running for president. Senator Kennedy and Vice President Nixon are."

"I know who's running for president," I said evenly. "And I don't think World War II is ever a side issue. For example, John Kennedy was a courageous World War II navy PT boat captain, who saved the lives of his entire crew after their boat was rammed by the Japanese."

"I am not interested in that right now," Teacher said sharply. "Now try to answer the question. What are the factors that qualify the very young and inexperienced John Kennedy to become the next president of the United States? And keep the war and the Jews out of it."

"Well," I said stubbornly, "I think World War II heroism is one factor. Kennedy kept his head after disaster struck. He had his men use their belts to tie themselves to a plank floating among the wreckage of their boat. That way no one who weakened could slip into the water and drown. How did he think of that? It's so simple and effective. Therefore, Kennedy is the man I'd want to have making decisions during a crisis."

"That's it?" Teacher snapped at me. "Tie yourself to a plank and then you win the presidential election? Is that all it takes?" she demanded.

It had been a long week, and I was feeling tired and out of sorts, so I said softly, "What are you afraid of? Are you trying to suppress a free exchange of ideas in the classroom? That seems unprofessional."

"Unprofessional?" Teacher said indignantly. Apparently, I wasn't the only one feeling tired and cranky.

"Could you ask someone else a question?" I said. "I don't have anything else to say. And I think the subject is irrelevant, because we're all too young to vote anyway."

Teacher didn't hide her annoyance. "Crosby, you've gone too far. You're being disrespectful. Now I don't want to hear any more sass from you." Her voice took on an angry, petulant note. "I run this class, and I'll decide what's relevant!"

Anger interests me. I watched Teacher to see how far her anger would take her. I had never seen her like this. She seemed to be boiling.

Now, with her face turning red and her voice suddenly rising in volume, she said harshly, "Crosby, like all the other teachers, I've put up with you and felt sorry for you and your mother, but you owe me an answer. Now, tell me what you think about Richard Nixon."

I'm no stranger when it comes to being yelled at. I associated raised voices, though, with drinking and the violence that follows.

Teacher was being very confrontational, and I didn't appreciate the low blow she had just delivered, but now I crossed a line into open defiance and contempt. "I know one thing for sure," I said shortly, "you're not being very nice to me today. Why don't you pick on someone else for a change?"

Teacher scowled furiously at me. She said in a threatening tone, "What did you just say to me, young man?" The rest of the class was stiff with silence. They stared at me and then at Teacher. Mostly, I felt confused and a little dazed. Had I caused all this? I could sense an ominous feeling hanging in the air.

But then another feeling swept over me. It began with a too-familiar upwelling of fear in my stomach, and to my horror, I knew what was about to happen. Tears burst out of my eyes, and I began to cry brokenly. I never wanted to weep; it just took me. I was ashamed when I cried and generally despised myself because of it, and I couldn't look anyone in the face for days afterward. I was analytical enough to wonder how such sobs could take me over and convulse my body, but I didn't know what mechanism would help me to stop.

Teacher, of course, changed her manner instantly. She seemed contrite and apologetic. She told me to go outside. I grabbed my crutches and went out the classroom door. All I needed was a few minutes to get control of myself. It would take a little longer, though, to bring my head up.

A few minutes later, Teacher joined me outside and spoke quickly and, I thought, rather impatiently to me. She said she knew what had happened to me and why I used crutches; I chose to ignore her claim. She said the principal would speak to me if I wanted to go to her office. That brought me up short. I began to staunch the flow of tears almost immediately. A trip to the principal's office was a very sobering thought. I had been there once already, and that was enough. The principal's office was a stark and forbidding place. All the furniture—her desk, two chairs, and one file cabinet—were gray metal. On one wall was a photograph of what must have been her family, and everybody was dressed in brown, standing rigidly and staring into the camera without the hint of a smile.

How a question about politics, asked on a gorgeous, sunny Friday in spring, could lead to this situation puzzled and perplexed me.

Teacher now gave me one last rather pitying look and went back into the classroom.

I didn't go to the principal's office. I calmed down and went back to my desk. Teacher was just concluding some instructions about A-bombs. She said we should duck and cover if we ever saw a bright flash of light, but I wasn't listening to her because a startling plan had begun to form in my mind. And the more I thought about it, the more excited I became.

The bell rang. Maria found me and offered to carry my books. She didn't say anything about what had happened in class, but I noticed her eyes were moist, and she didn't look directly at me. I felt sorry for her.

She was too emotional about things. My tears sort of tore out of me. I supposed that was upsetting to Maria, but I never considered those tears as my own. The cause of them eluded me, and I thought of them as invaders and strangers. It was that seemingly causeless outbreak of tears from somewhere deep within myself that confused me.

Teacher once wrote in the comments section of my report card: "Cries easily." When Mom read the two words, she told me quietly, "Tears are a language that Heaven understands."

Maybe so. But I didn't. My tears mostly made me feel angry and ashamed and emotionally frazzled.

All in all, I wondered what it would feel like to never have another outburst of crying. The plan I had thought of a few minutes ago began to take on definite shape. For the moment I let it form in all its perfection.

A few minutes later, Maria and I were walking down Orange Avenue, heading for our homes. To make conversation, I asked Maria if she ever went to church.

"Crosby, you know I'm Catholic. I go to mass every Sunday."

I told her I knew that. What I didn't say was that from time to time, I tried to forget it. Catholics weren't like what I was used to in religion. The fact was Catholics scared me because they drank real wine during a mass, and they also went to confession, where they had to tell a priest all about their sins.

Influencing my view of all Catholics was the Mazzoli family who lived next door to my church. They were solidly Catholic. The father was a plumber, and the mother was a small woman who never smiled. One of their two daughters was in my class at school. They were one of the many Italian families in Monte Vista. Mr. Mazzoli was huge and swarthy and strong and silent. Their home was rather small and always dimly lit at night. They never turned on a porch light, and any light coming from within the house was apparently produced by candles and not light bulbs.

I once had an encounter with Mr. Mazzoli. I was at Refredi's Market and I saw him pick up a gallon of port wine and then he stood right next to me at the meat counter. It was Gallo wine, and the jug was huge. The color of port wine is dark, dark red—just like old blood. No doubt Mr. Mazzoli was going to drink the whole jug that night. I often wondered what he had to say at confession. Probably that he enjoyed beating up small Protestant boys.

So there I was—respectful of Catholics because of Maria, but a little bit scared of them, too, because of Mr. Mazzoli.

Maria's street was only two blocks from school. I didn't know how anyone could live that close to school and not resent it. I was glad I lived eight blocks away. Our neighborhood was only about thirty or forty years old. There were no concrete sidewalks, just good old packed dirt, hard as stone, even when it rained.

And now before Maria turned down her street, I thought once more about the plan which had begun to form in my mind in class. I knew I could tell Maria. She would never laugh at me or betray me in any way.

So I took a deep breath and said firmly, "I'm not going to cry in class anymore. I've made up my mind. I'm done with that."

We were now standing at the corner of Orange Avenue and Alcazar Street. Maria's home was just a few houses down on the left. She was still carrying my books in the two-handled canvas bag I always used. She insisted on doing that for me every day. Then when we reached Alcazar Street, I always took the book bag and looped my arm through the two handles. After that, I let the bag hang loosely while I used my crutches and headed home.

Maria had just witnessed my outburst in class. It wasn't the first time I'd lost control like that. She was never ashamed or embarrassed by my tears. She was the one classmate who didn't make me feel like I should be hanging my head down in shame.

Now Maria smiled and said, "I cry sometimes too."

Well, maybe she did, but I'd never seen it. And I wasn't ready to ask Maria what she cried about. What if she told me? I didn't know if I could handle that. It could get a little sticky. That subject was more of a conversation for boyfriend and girlfriend, which we were not.

But in a strange way, Maria was the inspiration for my plan. I thought if she didn't turn on the waterworks in school, then why should I? Of course, I wasn't about to tell her that.

"I mean it," I said emphatically. "From now on, I'm going to be as dry-eyed as a turnip."

She looked at me with a certain calm on her face. "I'll see you on Monday, Crosby," she said lightly. And then she added, "I know you can do what you set your mind to. I'm confident of that."

I watched her as she turned down Alcazar Street, which wasn't much of a street name. It sounded too prison-like to me. The rest of the neighborhood streets, branching off of Orange Avenue, also had Spanish names. Names like: Lomita, San Fernando, Almaden, Hermosa, Granada. I loved saying the names. They all sounded dignified and elegant and regal.

I watched Maria a second longer and then turned toward home a mere six blocks away.

Mom, Grandma, and I lived in a good-sized white house on a piece of property at the corner of Orange Avenue and Granada Street. There was a small orchard of prune trees on one side of the house. Our landlord, who personally came to the house each month to collect the rent, never tended the orchard, but nevertheless each year, the trees yielded a small crop of prunes, which were not my favorite fruit. Other fruit trees grew around our house. There were fig, pomegranate, Japanese plum, walnut, almond, avocado, and orange trees. I wallowed in the abundance of free food at my fingertips. The Santa Clara Valley was truly sun-kissed and the soil was rich and productive. It seemed criminal that many of the orchards in the valley were now being uprooted to make way for Progress: more houses, more apartment complexes, more businesses, and more parking lots. Some progress!

There was a concrete walkway leading to our front steps. The front door opened on a rather large living room, otherwise known as doily land. Everything from the arms and backs of chairs, along with our sofa, coffee tables, and book cases—all were covered with a mantle of Grandma's hand-sewn, intricately patterned white doilies. On the walls were framed photographs of relatives, many of whom I had never known. Also a funeral home calendar, given out free each year in church—as though death were so near and dear, you had to have the funeral parlor's telephone number memorized—was hung prominently on a rusty nail near the kitchen door. Off the living room were two rather narrow bedrooms with a small bathroom between them.

There was a swinging door between the living room and the spacious kitchen, which was dominated by a large stove and several mismatched chairs arranged around the kitchen table. The table was situated in the sunniest corner, allowing streams of California sunlight to regularly pour into the room.

But like Br'er Rabbit, I had a special place, not for laughing, but for reading and thinking. It was an L-shaped enclosed back porch, which ran most of the length of both the back of the house and the side of the house that looked out on the prune orchard. It appeared to me that at one point in the past, the porch had been added on to the main house to provide a place to sit in the cool of the day. It was here when we moved in, and Mom and Grandma had more or less yielded it to me. I had made it into my domain. It was my theater of action. There were three double beds, all nearly buried under Grandma's hand-sewn patchwork quilts, arranged along the outside walls. Curtained windows dominated the upper portion of the full length of both walls. There were three entrances to the porch. One entrance was off the kitchen, near the washing machine, and the huge washtub in the corner. There was a pair of glass-paneled double doors off the living room. I could go through those doors and crawl into bed after a satisfying evening of reading or watching *Wagon Train* or *Maverick* or *Sugarfoot*. The third door led to the outside. It was blocked a little by one of the beds. It opened onto a genuine greenhouse where Grandma started her tomatoes and flowers in the early spring. I could get in and out of the house through the greenhouse door if I heaved myself at it with all my sixty-five pounds, which wasn't much of a heave, but at least I could squeeze through.

The back porch—the only name we used for this wing of the house—was used as a catchall. Boxes of cast-off clothing, donated pieces of unmatched furniture, all of which were dented and scratched and showing places where the varnish was chipped away were scattered here and there. There was a nightstand of dark mahogany—old, ornate, and unusable—for one of the legs was missing. We had a dented and scarred bookcase that had jars of home-canned jellies, jams, and preserves on the shelves.

And among all these randomly scattered pieces of furniture where many hiding places, for I had items that had to be kept from view. I had a chest of drawers for my clothes, which were always folded neatly and then carefully put away, but I never hid anything in those drawers. The risk of discovery was too high. Not that Grandma and Mom were nosy, it's just that a man has to exercise reasonable caution when hiding his secret stuff. No, for that there was an imposing cabinet, five feet high and just as wide. It had ruined hinges and two doors that sagged when opened. It was a nuisance to open, and so we just let it sit there unused. Except I knew how to get the cabinet doors opened and clicked shut without so much as a whisper of sound. It was the perfect cache for all my paperbacks.

So you might say that the house on Orange Avenue was a home with attitude, if not outright personality. It rang with a sense of history—how did it get here and who had built it and who had lived in it over the years? Perhaps some wealthy bootleggers, fat cat bankers, shyster lawyers, corrupt politicians, washed-up movie stars? But putting all that aside, what was more engaging to me was the fact that right now one Plunk and two Hoggards inhabited the place.

Grandma Plunk, who had been living with us for three years, was a unique personality in our home on Orange Avenue. Grandma had her own expressive manner. She said words deliberately, like they were events. She probably missed her calling—she should have been an orator or a poetess. She used words like they were weapons. She didn't say that much, preferring to defer to my mother's judgment at home, but when she spoke, I generally listened. She always told me her calling was to her grandchildren. And by that she meant the calling of God. I liked to be near her when she was ironing clothes, but I was a little intimidated by the things she told me. I didn't want a catalog of Grandma's sayings in my head. Her sayings tried to push my stories away. Sometimes in the middle of remembering how an unknown, unexpected spring of pure water had burst forth from the miserable earth of Andersonville Prison, I'd recall Grandma telling me that God told my Mom to name me Crosby. That was a good one. If only God had told her to change our last name to Smith or Jones—now that would have been something grand. But Hoggard? I had a nickname. At school, the well-known corpulent playground bully, Clyde Winston, liked to call me Singing Pig, a cheap and tiresome play on my Bing Crosbyish first name and the hoggishness in my last name. Clyde's brain was stunted to say the best about him, which I never did. When he wasn't calling me names, Clyde was busy flunking everything in sight. He'd already failed second and fourth grades. I don't know why the school officials didn't just get it over with and send him to reform school, his life's destiny as far as I could see.

Even though I never told Mom or Grandma about nicknames, I think they must have guessed. Once Grandma told me never to worry about being called names. She said Joseph's brothers hated him and gave him the nickname of the Dreamer. Then they sold him into slavery. Of course later, Joseph was made number 2 man in Egypt and eventually saved the lives of all his family. I thought about that. If I were ever made the number 2 man in Egypt, I think I'd have Clyde Winston arrested and charged with multiple felony counts of being a bully. Then I'd have him tried and convicted and sentenced to life imprisonment at hard labor: with one chubby hand tied behind his back, he'd have to build a pyramid by himself. And then after the pyramid was constructed, I'd let him eat.

There was one thing that Grandma didn't know I was fully aware of. Grandma watched her plays on television every day. She wasn't exactly proud of watching them. In fact, she was downright secretive about it, so she never talked about the plots or characters.

She gave the impression that her plays were not worth her time—the storylines were dopey and crude and maudlin and sometimes rather seamy—and I judged that as a Christian woman she didn't want to be entertained by other people and their wicked lives. But apart from all the game shows—which she told me featured nothing but human greed—the only thing on TV in the afternoon were her plays.

Once when I was home sick from school, I could hear the TV from my room, and Grandma, except for the time she was tending to me, never missed a word. She never referred to the afternoon programs as soap operas, only as plays. It was her and Mom's worst kept little secret.

You would have thought that watching all those TV plays would have ruined her mind by now. I had seen a few of the programs and thought the stories were shallow, teary, and silly. So I figured that Grandma was not exactly hearing the actor's words. Perhaps she was just praying for those poor plagued people.

The Plunks were generally blondish and blue-eyed and blessed with an iron constitution. There was very little sickness among them. It must have been the hard work that did it. Grandma and her daughters, including my mother, were not unacquainted with working long hours at physically demanding work. Grandma herself was slender and sprightly and strong and always as busy as a cat with its fur on fire. She had piercing blue eyes and always wore plain dresses around the house. It was dresses only. Grandma wore no manner of jeans or long pants as a rule.

It must have been a generational thing, because my Mom wore pants regularly to work. She was like her sisters, the same blue eyes, and she was talkative, kind, and caring. But she was my Mom, and therefore, she had always been there, infinite and wise and rather unknowable, but definitely imposing and sometimes unpredictable.

My mother worked two days a week at Collier's Cannery, which was only three blocks away, over on Imperial Avenue. She canned prunes most of the year and, beginning in August, worked very long hours canning tomatoes from early morning to dark. Sometimes she didn't get home till nine or ten o'clock at night during tomato season, for since it was seasonal work, the tomatoes had to be canned then and there and not left over to the next day. Her income increased dramatically during tomato season because she was then working six days a week. But the season only lasted about five weeks, and then it was back to prunes and only two days of work per week, requiring her to ride the bus from Monte Vista to the Santa Clara County Unemployment Office in downtown San Jose.

Our rent was seventy dollars a month, an enormous figure to me. I worried too much about whether we could pay it. I wanted a job so I could help out at home, but what kind of job could a seventh grader find? A paper route? It would take me forever to deliver all the papers. Every few weeks, concern about money matters would menace my mind so much that I had to stop thinking about it or I'd go crazy with worry.

But at those times my books were a great help to me. When I was wrapped up in Wang Lung's troubles in China, or Francie and Neeley's troubles in Brooklyn, my troubles seemed trivial in comparison. They didn't exactly go away, but I could replace my worried thoughts with something else. Sometimes church sermons helped to get my mind thinking differently too, but usually I went back to my books for help. My books, I suppose, were like Grandma's plays. The plots and subplots of other people's lives were earthshaking and profound and entertaining and more important than the storyline of my bookish, ordinary, and rather insignificant life.

I had read many books that Mom and Grandma knew nothing about. I had read all about wicked and disgraceful relationships between men and women; I knew about murders and suicides and treason and assassinations and greed and theft and other dangerous human deviations. I read about delusions, aberrations, and fiendish behaviors. There were many seamy things going on in my books and in my mind, I admitted that much myself, because I read books in which the Ten Commandments were regularly broken, especially commandments numbers 1 and 2 and 6, 7, and 8. I sometimes wondered what my church would think if they knew what kind of books I was reading. But they'd never know, because I wasn't about to tell them. Then again, the Old Testament wasn't exactly free from an assortment of sordid stories in which the Ten Commandments were violated, ignored, and stomped on. King David not only committed adultery and got Bathsheba pregnant, but he also fiendishly with malice aforethought arranged for her husband, Uriah, to be killed. That story made me very angry. How could David be that stupid? It's a good thing he repented of his sin, or I wouldn't like him at all.

Sometimes you have to dig long and hard to get to the gold. My books were like that. I always read a book from cover to cover, and I had learned how to swallow the meat and spit out the bones, meaning that among the jumble of things that took place in my books— from one end of that particular spectrum to the other—there were some dazzling flashes of majestic light along the way. For instance, I observed how Francie Nolan, with the help of her doomed alcoholic father's help, was able to attend a better school in Brooklyn. I struggled along with Lucas Marsh as he overcame insuperable odds and became a doctor; I stood up solidly—shoulder to shoulder— with other prisoners and refused to let the cruelties of Andersonville Prison break my mind and spirit, I knew how HMJFC fooled the British military and got three hundred children on board the ship *Exodus*. And best of all, I had witnessed Dov Landau beating the murderous Nazi system in the Warsaw Ghetto. When I grow up, I want to be a forger of documents by day and then at night make my way through the ghetto sewer system to the city outside the ghetto walls. There I would secure desperately needed supplies for those still trapped inside the ghetto. I wanted to set prisoners free. I wanted to be a member of the Hagganah or the Palmach or the Aliyah Bet or the Maccabees and help oppressed people.

My imagination flamed and soared with brave people in books. I wanted to travel Route 66 from Oklahoma to California with the Joads, and I wanted to buy a genuine grass skirt from Bloody Mary on some South Pacific island for fo' dolla'. A boring sermon was endurable when I occupied my mind with Laurel, Floral, Zoral, and Coral, all of whom lived near Andersonville Prison and had a pet: a dead chicken which they dragged around on a string.

It didn't matter if school gave me the Treatment, because nothing could break me if I knew how not to listen. And with my head full of the greatest characters ever written about, I could endure whatever slings and arrows were aimed at me. If my friend Dov Landau could survive Auschwitz, I could survive anything. A man has to have his role models, and I had mine.

Grandma had a habit each day of meeting me at the door when I got home from school. And true to form, she had been there this afternoon and had asked me her usual question.

"How did you do today, Crosby?" she asked with a smile.

"I had a great day and learned a lot," I said breezily, hoping my superficial answer had satisfied her.

She always wanted to know about my friends, as though I had quite a few. It seemed a mystery to her, my life and adventures. But most of the time I gave her sparing details and a generally lame accounting of my day. That was because I didn't know how she would respond to a real telling of how I got my nickname or what I had said in class that day. Judging by appearances, Grandma seemed some-how anxious about me, and I had learned that if I mentioned one odd detail to her, it would open the door for a new round of several pointed questions. I felt it was safest to let my life as a sleeping dog just lie there without comment.

Therefore, I was rather closemouthed about my hours at school, as well as about my reading. I, more or less, kept those two things to myself. Grandma didn't need to worry about me. Didn't she know I could take care of myself? Was it my crutches? Crutch or no crutch, I was self-sufficient. Compared to the horrors of what the Nazis did to Dov Landau's family, my crutches were negligible. And that's how I regarded the situation. I treated my need for crutches as if it were a short-lived hindrance. My brain and my soul were untouched.

Besides, I had a suspicion I was getting better. My feet and legs weren't as bad as they used to be. I kept it to myself, though. I wasn't ready for the fame my church would try to put on me. They'd call it a miracle and trumpet the news and parade me around and demand that I testify about how God had healed me. If God was going to fix my body, he could do it slowly behind the scenes, and then it would come about so gradually that nobody would notice.

Grandma was usually satisfied with my rather shallow answers to her afternoon question, but today, she startled me with some rather shocking news.

"Dad Upland will be preaching this Sunday morning!" she said, her face shining with happiness.

The name had a curious force over me. Grandma had been telling me stories about Dad Upland for years. In fact, I regarded the events of Dad's life as my favorite bedtime stories. I was not raised on tales of wolves wearing grandma's clothes or witches trying to bake and eat children or old ladies living in a shoe. It was Bible stories and Dad Upland stories I had heard.

"How long will he stay this time?" I asked. Sometimes Dad preached several nights in a row; other times he preached Sunday and was gone the next day.

Grandma looked at me curiously. "Only the Lord knows the answer to that question."

Dad Upland came and went. Other visiting preachers were announced well in advance, but Dad you heard about when he drove into town, always without so much as a phone call to anyone. He was probably eighty-five years old and thin as a rail. He drove a Chevrolet, the only automobile he trusted.

Overall I had sketchy memories of Dad Upland in person. I'd only heard him preach a time or two, and I might have even talked with him once, but those memories were a little fuzzy. I do recall that his sermons tended to take detours and ramble over several topics. It didn't matter what theme he started on, he always roamed around in many directions.

I'd like to think that I have a wide breadth of knowledge and a finely honed intuitive and logical grasp of many ideas. For instance, I'm a man of science—I've read all about the voyage of the Kon – Tiki, and I believe in Univac; I'm a man of letters—I've studied Zane Grey and Dostoyevsky; I'm a man of appetites—every once in a while, when Mom and Grandma aren't looking, I sneak into the kitchen and toss back three fingers of red wine vinegar, which hits my palate with a rosy liquid burst of piquant burning flavor; and I'm a man of culture—I am fascinated by Dali's melting watches, and I know several Spanish swear words. My grasp of the meaning of life and death and suffering has been thought out in detail. Therefore, if anyone can follow the direction of a sermon, I'm that person. But with Dad, the content and thrust of his sermons left me thrown off-balance, a little perplexed, and sometimes stranded somewhere out in the South 40. Still, after he preached, you felt edified. Dad never said a harsh word about anyone. He preached like he understood us, and he never gave anyone a bawling out. Grandma said that when he finished a sermon, you knew that everything was going to turn out all right. I always liked that thought—everything was going to somehow turn out all right— it's just that I wanted more proof than a sermon for the sentiment.

I usually read one or two hours when I came home from school, and most evenings after dinner, I watched a little TV in the living room with Mom and Grandma. Tonight was no exception, and when I began to nod off, I got up from the couch and went out to the back porch to get ready for bed.

There was only one other citizen in my kingdom. His name was Beatnik, a well-muscled orange tabby cat. He was a proud, independent, freedom-loving creature, who more or less put up with me. He had his own double bed, but most of the time, he slept at the foot of my bed, that is to say, when he was around.

He had his moods. And one of them was that he liked to go away for a day or two and then come home to me like nothing out of the ordinary had happened. Some mornings he was out prowling before I was awake, and at night I could feel him pounce on my bed if he thought I was too comfortable. He needed me to scratch behind his ears and feed him leftovers. We couldn't afford the luxury of buying cat food at Refredi's Market, but Beatnik had his own diet. He was a skilled hunter and generally consumed only one-half of his quarry. It was usually half a mouse or half a bird. The other half he left on my bed, thus proving his prowess and his worth to me.

He was pugnacious and defiant at times, but more often than not, we got along. There was something so independent about Beatnik that half the time I envied him and felt happy that he had wandered around our door one day and then adopted me as his associate. I didn't own him. He owned me and favored me with his formidable presence.

He suffered from oil stains. Beatnik regularly rolled around under the cars in the neighborhood and then, smelling of a fresh coating of dirt and oil, plunked himself down on his bed. He would then stretch himself out elegantly and, licking his paws with a Brillo Pad-like tongue, proceed to scrub himself clean from top to bottom. He had no visible means of support, lived off the goodness of others, had no interest in full-time work, and generally lazed around: hence, the name Beatnik.

I gathered Beatnik up in my arms. Our agreement was that he allowed me to hold him as long as I immediately found a particular favorite spot on his neck or behind his ears and began to scratch carefully and energetically. He resented clumsy treatment and now and then took a few swipes at me if I was too rough or too slow in catching onto his particular needs at that moment.

Grandma told me once that Beatnik was like the brother I never had, and that I should stop imitating his behavior. She warned me to stay out from under the neighbor's cars because she couldn't spend all day washing oil stains off Beatnik's bedding and mine also. She was smiling when she said it, and I assured her earnestly that I never actually rolled in oil under any cars; I was just checking the mufflers for damage.

Today had been eventful. I meant what I had resolved: I wasn't going to break out in tears anymore. I was getting sleepy now, and I thought fleetingly that I was glad I had told Maria. She was a good witness, and I now had someone to prove myself to. I thought of my resolution as a sort of personal experiment, and I wanted to discover what would happen if I applied myself to such a project.

Beatnik jumped out of my arms and leaped over to his own bed, where he curled up in a tight orange ball.

I had been in school all day, and I had missed the Nolan children. They made me happy. They were very poor, but they made do with what they had. They lived in Brooklyn, and their father was a singing waiter. Francie and Neeley helped me unwind. I was smiling when I opened the book. It's words plunged me into another world.

But after a few minutes of reading, I began to yawn hugely. I fought sleep off for a time. I just wanted to finish a few more pages, but sleep always wins out. I reached over and turned off my bedside lamp. I pulled the quilts up under my chin, and, thinking at the last second about how pretty Maria's smile had been today, I dropped off to sleep.

* * * * *

-SATURDAY-

The next morning I woke up abruptly, and after a few minutes, I was relieved to discover that I could not remember last night's dreams. Someone told me once that the secret to remembering dreams was to concentrate on them the instant you woke up, and then you could write them down. Therefore, I reasoned, the opposite must also be true: don't ever concentrate on them and definitely don't commit any dreams to paper—they might crawl off the page someday and come shambling after you with a grating, mewling cry. My dreams were a jumbled-up hair-raising assortment of full color images that made me sweat. And by virtue of the technique of not concentrating, I usually couldn't recall my dreams. However, every now and then, a vivid dream would violate my rule and come plummeting into my mind. It was always the same: I was falling or I was looking over a cliff and then was shoved from behind or I was trying to get away from something sinister, but I was being slowly overtaken.

So I had learned to never concentrate on my dreams and even laugh at them, and by using these techniques, I had no unpleasant dreams to dwell on most of the time.

Saturday was my day. Mom and Grandma cleaned the house, did the laundry, mopped the floors, and, in general, prepared for Sunday on Saturday.

I was mostly exempt from house chores, and it was understood that Saturday belonged to me. And today was one I had been looking forward to for some time. My mother's three sisters were coming over for dessert tonight. It would be another in a long series of conversations from which I had been learning about my family history, including boatloads of racy details I wasn't supposed to hear.

But this morning, I had plenty to occupy my time. First, I had biscuits and eggs and bacon for breakfast, and to officially celebrate the fact that it was Saturday, I had a half a cup of black coffee because Francie and Neeley had convinced me that a little coffee was just fine for children. Second, I was going downtown for a haircut which meant I could try once again to talk to Abraham Greenberg about Dov Landau.

The other main activity for me today was the acquisition of a new stash of paperbacks. Good old Aunt Zonell would come through again, and I wondered how we would affect the transfer tonight.

After breakfast I read for a couple of hours. Now and then, Mom had talked to me about the importance of having a daily devotional time alone with God and my Bible. I had observed her with her well-worn Bible every morning for as long as I could remember. She also had a promise box shaped like a tiny loaf of bread. It contained Bible verses printed on thick pieces of colored paper. There were ninety-five promises in the box. I knew this because I used to count them all the time after tossing them into the air. Grandma thought it was scandalous to treat God's word so recklessly, but Mom always defended me.

"It's not as though he's throwing the Bible," she used to say. "At least he's got some of God's word in his hands."

The fact was that I read my own assortment of materials for my devotional time. It was always profitable to read about my friend Dov or Francie and Neeley or Anthony Adverse or Jody and Fodderwing. They were all so inspiring and strong and fearless.

Some mornings, when I came into the kitchen, Mom would ask me how my devotional time went.

"It was just great," I would tell her. "The people I read about are so brave, and they do wonderful things that inspire me to live a life of faith and courage, and I can learn from the mistakes of those who made bad choices. I feel humble just thinking about it."

Mom always beamed with pleasure at my words. Of course, she thought I meant people like David and Samuel and Paul the Apostle, but I had usually just spent consecrated time with Scarlett and Rhett or Ari Ben Canaan or Ma Joad. At other times, I devoted with Laurel, Floral, Coral, and Zoral or Lucas Marsh or Jaimie McPheeters. I didn't ignore David and Samuel and Paul, I just knew that on Sunday I would probably hear all about them anyway. But no one was going to preach about Dov Landau, so it was left up to me to extract lessons from his life.

And this morning, Abraham Greenberg had been on my mind as I read about how the Danes had shipped the Jews out of Denmark to safety rather than hand them over to the Nazis. And good King Christian had made a radio speech in which he told the people of his country that one Dane was exactly the same as the next Dane, and that he, King Christian—in response to the German order that all Jews must wear a yellow star of David—would wear the armband, and he expected every loyal Dane to do the same. And they all did!

I couldn't read such accounts without my heart pounding with excitement. Such a brave nation, such a brave people. I supposed that Abraham Greenberg knew all about this, because he was Jewish and very old and had lived through World War II.

He was also my barber and seldom said more than two words when he cut my hair. Today, though, I was going to get him talking.

By midmorning, I considered that I had read enough. I knew that Abraham and Yetta's Variety Store and Barber Shop was open by now. The Greenbergs had been in Monte Vista ever since the days when it was something of a summer resort for folks from San Francisco who would take a special train south from the city to get to their weekend cottages here.

But sadly, Monte Vista's resort days were over. Mom said no one had exactly abandoned Monte Vista, but the families who could afford to had migrated to larger homes in Cupertino and other out-lying suburbs, leaving the families here somewhat isolated and living in rather tight quarters.

And no matter how Abraham and Yetta Greenberg had got here, they had carved out a place for themselves in the community as the owners of the only variety store in town. But speech seemed hard for them. It was nearly impossible to get words out of Abraham. I knew two things about Abraham and Yetta: they were Jewish, and they came from San Francisco to Monte Vista about thirty years ago. Other than that, I was left to wonder. Did they attend synagogue somewhere? Had they ever been to Israel? Did they have relatives in Europe who had experienced persecution during World War II? And most importantly, could they introduce me to Dov Landau or Ari Ben Canaan?

Mom gave me a dollar and two dimes. The dollar was for the haircut, and the dimes were for candy.

My haircuts used to be taken care of at home, for in the past Grandma had cut my hair. But over time, her hands had slowly become more and more unsteady, and I had begun to dread the thought of losing an ear or an eye due to her shaky hands. When I realized the possibility of falling victim to her scissors, I began to hide them around the house. At first, Grandma thought she had misplaced them, but then I'd begin to feel guilty and I'd hand them over to her after making an ostentatious display of finding them. So Grandma always got her scissors back, and after taking them in her jittery hands, I would once again be subjected to a wobbly hair-cutting ordeal.

Thankfully, after a time, Mom began to notice little clumps of hair here and there on my scalp which unexpectedly stood up and nearly waved hello. She got the message even though no words passed between us, and we reached a compromise: Mom somehow convinced Grandma to retire from the hair-cutting business and now as the need arose, I went to Abraham and Yetta's for a haircut and got candy money to boot.

Mom was always a little wary whenever I went to Abraham and Yetta's. So when I was standing at the front door, ready to go, Mom said, "Crosby, you sit real still in the barber chair while Abraham cuts your hair." There was real concern in her voice.

"I'll be all right," I said confidently. "I know how to get along with Abraham." It's a man's job to soothe the worries of anxious mothers, and I was quick to help my Mom with her unnecessary concern.

"Abraham can be awfully grouchy sometimes," she added uneasily.

"Not with me," I answered. "I do all the talking, and I think he likes me."

I went out and closed the door behind me. Any Saturday in spring smells good. The sun wasn't blistering hot, but it was beginning to warm up, and I could feel the warmth on my face.

I could never get enough of our front yard. We had two orange trees, a walnut tree, a Japanese plum tree, and an almond tree, and that was just in our front yard. The fig trees and the Granny Smith Apple tree and the pomegranate tree were out back. The smells of blossoms and resins surrounded me like scents from Heaven.

From our front yard, I headed diagonally across a vacant lot on the corner to Skylar's Texaco gas station. We lived one house away from Steven's Creek Boulevard, an imposing name for a simple two-lane road. Beyond the Texaco Service Station was Abraham and Yetta's store on the corner. This was downtown Monte Vista. It wasn't like Francie and Neeley's Brooklyn, but just the same, I liked my serene Saturdays here.

I was using my one crutch with great skill. Grandma was the one growing shakier, but I was getting stronger and stronger every day in my feet and legs. I had decided this morning that I wasn't going to use two crutches anymore. From now on, it was one crutch only.

I easily went up the two steps using the handrail and walked inside the store. There was a glass-topped counter on the left near the door. And perched on it was a huge cash register. There were only two aisles in the store, and both were very narrow, the shelves rising up nearly to the ceiling, as if Abraham and Yetta had tried to stock as much merchandise as possible on the shelves. A tall revolving metal paperback book display rack stood at attention near the front door. I wanted every book for my own.

The barber chair was in back where Abraham usually sat when he wasn't cutting hair. Yetta evidently ran the store, while her husband read the newspaper, smoked smelly black cigars, and listened to classical music on the radio.

Mrs. Abraham Greenberg wore faded flower-patterned dresses day in and day out. Once perhaps, her dresses had been yellow or gold or orange, but now all of them were an indifferent dingy gold, like faded royalty. There was something queenly about Yetta. She carried herself with dignity, a gentle composure that brought her respect. She must have been the glue that held everything together because it was well known that Abraham was grouchy and abrupt, and on his bad days, he was irritable, mean, and quarrelsome. I was hoping for the former today. Mom had been right. Abraham twisted heads roughly when cutting hair. He would bark, "Head up" or "Head down" at the customer without any particular knowledge of who it was in his chair. We were all just disembodied heads of overgrown hair to him.

But today I was going to engage him in conversation. I made my way to the back of the store.

Abraham looked up from his paper, and there I was standing in front of him, leaning on one crutch. He folded the paper without saying one word to me, brushed the cigar ashes off his stained white shirt, and grabbed a towel from a rack on the wall. There was a door behind him, and it was slightly ajar, allowing a little air in the store.

I hadn't moved. "How are you today, Mr. Greenberg?" I asked pleasantly.

He gave me an absent look. I knew that to him, I was just another little kid getting a haircut, but today, I was going to break through that invisible barrier.

"Get in the chair," he grunted, his voice raspy and disinterested.

"Sure, Mr. Greenberg," I said promptly. "I think I'd like the usual trim." I propped my crutch against the wall behind the barber chair and sat down. Abraham then stepped on a pedal at the base of the chair, and I began to ascend one click at a time.

I was feeling alert and confident now, I was a paying customer and therefore he owed me communication.

Mr. Greenberg, a scowl on his face, began to clip at my hair with a pair of long pointed scissors. He always cut the front first, so he was standing in front of me, combing my hair down and then cutting it slantwise across my forehead. His eyes saw only my hair. I noticed the thin wrinkles around his eyes and the dark smudges under them. There were dull brown flecks in his irises, and he smelled of some aftershave or barber lotion that reminded me of a doctor's office. His face was thin and bony, and he was a little stoop-shouldered. I had never seen him smile.

I wanted to break his concentration and get his attention.

"Did you know you are the apple of God's eye?" I asked respectfully.

He evidently didn't hear me, for he kept cutting my hair, and the scowl never left his face. He was being careful with the way he transferred the scissors and comb back and forth between hands. My hair had his full attention, not the question I'd just asked him.

So I repeated it.

He moved behind me and barked, "Head down." Still no response to my question. I was prompt, and my head was down immediately. I didn't want him angry or impatient with me. I was still hoping to open the lines of communication. The teachers at school talked and jabbered all day long, and I usually listened with one ear. And now here I was trying to get Mr. Greenberg to open up, and I was afraid he was only half-listening to me. But he wouldn't say a thing, and I really wanted to get some thoughts out of him.

I wasn't going to be put off, for I had another device. "You have a fascinating first name, Mr. Greenberg," I began. "In fact, I was just reading recently about Abraham in the Holy Scriptures. How do you suppose a man feels who fathers a child when he is ninety-nine years old?"

"Head up," he ordered.

I was getting a little desperate now. When Mr. Greenberg was finished with my hair, that was when he was finished with me. Customers at Abraham and Yetta's paid Yetta up front. When Mr. Greenberg concluded a haircut, he always sat back down in the vacant barber chair and resumed reading and cigar smoking. He never said "Thank you" or "See you next time."

"Do you believe in God, Mr. Greenberg?" I asked. I wanted to be sure he understood I wasn't trying to put him on some embarrassing spot, so I added, "I believe in God, but I feel there is so much suffering and tragedy and injustice and death on the earth that you have to try to hang on to what little faith you can."

"I don't know what you mean," he said brusquely. "You be still, and I'll be done soon. Don't talk anymore."

He lathered me up around each ear and used a straight razor to shave over them. He wiped off the leftover shaving cream with a paper towel and then with his knee, nudged the chair around to face the mirror.

"Okay?" he asked. I'm sure he expected me to answer in the affirmative.

But I had to get to the bottom of things. "I know you're Jewish, Mr. Greenberg," I said earnestly. "I've read about how the Jews were treated in Europe during World War II and how Hitler murdered six million Jews in his ovens. I know about that. It's the only thing I listen to in school. I have a heart too, and I cry sometimes when I think about how I'd feel if some Nazi with a machinegun gave me a bar of soap and told me I'd get my work assignment after I took a shower and then they'd slam the door shut, but it wasn't a shower. It was a gas chamber, and the bar of soap was made out of stone. And maybe my Mom and Grandma would be torn away from me because somebody thinks we're the wrong religion or the wrong race."

I definitely had Mr. Greenberg's attention now. I was facing the large mirror, and its reflection, I could see his face—suffused now with angry red patches—glaring steadily and wide-eyed at me. His raspy voice was flat and final and agitated when he spoke.

"You get out of my chair and my store and never come back!" he said coldly. "What do you know of such things?" He was breathing hard and speaking louder than I'd ever heard him speak.

"I know about suffering and death," I plunged on. "My religion is eccentric and controversial, Mr. Greenberg. People talk about us. If the Jewish people could be singled out, then we're next. It's all connected. That's why I love you and Mrs. Greenberg, because I think you're both brave and noble, and someday I'm going to Israel and live and work at a Kibbutz."

He said vehemently, "This I do not want to hear. Now go!"

I began to get up, but there was one thing I had forgotten: that ratcheting sound I'd heard when I first sat down meant that the barber chair had risen. So now as I stepped down to the level where the wooden floor had always been, I discovered it wasn't there at all. I grabbed for the arm of the chair about one beat too late. I fell forward. There was enough space between the chair and the wall for me to hit the floor and not knock anything over. I rolled over and sat up. Falling isn't new to me. You don't use crutches as long as I have and not take an occasional tumble or two. And as far as injuries from falling go, this one was nothing. I didn't make much noise either.

Abraham was standing still, gaping and glaring at me. My crutch had fallen near me. I picked it up and got to my feet and only noticed then that Yetta was standing there. The commotion from my fall and Mr. Greenberg's rising voice, no doubt, had gotten her attention.

"So, are you happy now?" she demanded, staring accusingly at her husband.

Abraham didn't look at Yetta. "Both of you, get out!" he said hoarsely.

I felt a brief explanation was in order. "It was all my fault, Mrs. Greenberg. I should have been more careful."

Yetta hadn't moved. Her expression was sad and troubled, her eyes filled with a pain I couldn't put my finger on.

No one spoke for a moment. Abraham was standing at the door behind the barber chair. He wouldn't look at me or his wife. Mrs. Greenberg was still staring at her husband. And I was thinking that I didn't want to be the cause of a domestic dispute.

At last I found my voice. "As you can both see, there was no harm done," I insisted quietly. "I apologize for my fall."

"You did nothing to apologize for," Mrs. Greenberg said not looking at me. Instead she was giving her husband a piercing stare.

And then she said something to Mr. Greenberg, an entire sentence in another language. Her voice rose as she spoke. She sounded like she was explaining something important to him. What surprised me the most was hearing her distinctly saying my name in the midst of all those strange-sounding foreign words.

But stranger still was Mr. Greenberg's reaction. He looked at me curiously, his manner becoming rather subdued. He said, "I did not know. Crosby Hoggard from the newspaper." He turned and walked out the door.

My mind was working as I watched him leave. He did not know what? He knew my name? And why was my name mentioned in a newspaper?

I was puzzled by Mr. Greenberg's words, but I had no time to ponder them, because Mrs. Greenberg now turned and went out to the cash register. I had a haircut to pay for, so I followed behind her. And after selecting a Milky Way and a Mounds candy bar, I put my money on the counter.

And as Mrs. Greenberg rang up one haircut and two candy bars, I thought of a certain question I was burning to ask her.

When she took my money, I said, "If I was to write a letter to Dov Landau, do you think he would receive it by next week?"

She gave me a blank look. "Who is this Dov Landau?"

"You know. The Dov Landau who had his fourteenth birthday at Auschwitz. Then he went to Palestine after the war and helped resettle the land." I told her it was all written down in black and white and pointed to the exact paperback in the revolving stand near the door. I had my facts down. I had read the book three times. Dov was probably a national hero by now and receiving bags of letters from schoolchildren and well-wishers from all over the world.

Mrs. Greenberg gave me a quizzical look, and then something like understanding touched her features. "No such person exists," she said flatly. "Yes, I know the name now. It is all pretend. You must never come here again and speak of these painful things. You are a small boy with too many thoughts."

"But I study about your people and about how nations make agreements with Israel and then break their word almost immediately," I said earnestly. "I don't want the Jewish people shoved into the Mediterranean Sea."

She snapped the cash register drawer shut and handed me a few cents. "This is not a thing I care to speak about."

"I can understand that—the pain, I mean," I said evenly. "But I want you to know that none of those things will ever happen again as long as I have breath in my body, because I'm on your side. And I'm leaving now. Remember: next year in Jerusalem. Shalom," I said, waving goodbye.

I stuffed the cash register receipt in my pocket as I left the store, thinking about the pain that some people have to live with. It made whatever pain I had more bearable by comparison. I would need to learn understanding and compassion. Suppose it was my relatives who had died at Auschwitz, I thought. How would I feel if I was living with that knowledge and then some skinny kid came to me and wanted to talk about it like it was all over and done away with? Some things never go away, and I was determined to learn how to talk to people about those terrible situations. Bottling things up doesn't work. I thought of Mr. Greenberg—he was holding so much in that he had to run out the back door rather than talk about it. My goal was to uncork the bottles and let the fizz out gracefully.

Mom and Grandma were always interested in my haircuts and made a fuss over me when I got home.

"Well now, Crosby," Mom said when she looked me over. "You look like a senator."

I told her that insults weren't going to get her anywhere.

"And how was Mr. Greenberg?" Grandma asked a little anxiously.

"He was unusually talkative today," I said seriously. "In fact, he's never spoken so much to me. I think I'm softening him up. We had a short but lively conversation that among other things touched on the life of Abraham, personal suffering, and eccentric religions."

The three of us were standing in the living room. I was still feeling quite exhilarated by the morning activities, but for some reason, Mom and Grandma, their heads tilted to one side, were staring rather quizzically at me.

It was now a little after twelve, and I wanted to hit the books a few minutes before lunch. I went out on the back porch. Beatnik was nowhere to be found, which didn't surprise me. Most days he roamed and ranged around the neighborhood and then sauntered home in time for leftovers and a quick scratching behind the ears, followed by some bed rest.

I deftly opened the book cabinet with the ruined hinges and selected a book. I sat down and read about Francie and Neeley's father, so handsome, so talented, and so doomed. I wanted their father to live, but the Nolan men all died young. And when Mr. Nolan died, he left a grieving widow and two orphans behind. I remembered studying about knights last year in school and how part of their Code of Chivalry was to protect widows and orphans, but nobody protected Francie and Neeley. They collected rags and shiny gum wrapper papers each week just to sell them for a few cents on Saturdays. But that's what happens to orphans who aren't cared for. I wanted to be Sir Crosby, protector of widows and orphans. My Code of Chivalry would include teaching them how to live, and then they wouldn't have to worry about paying the rent on time or having enough food on the table, and the orphans wouldn't have to worry about being robbed of a father and all the lessons you were supposed to learn from a father's heart and the warm security you'd feel from a father's strong, loving hugs.

I've noticed that interesting conversations, like the ones I had this morning with Abraham and Yetta, can expend a lot of energy. I felt like a lumberjack after a double shift. I was spent and worn out. But I knew what to do about it. I put the book away.

I got up and went out the back door of the porch to the prune orchard. Getting back to nature provides a bridge to revitalization of creative juices. I was feeling drained. I walked among the trees, feeling the hard earth under my feet. The gnarled trees looked wonderful. Each one had its own character and identity. They were like bony old guardians of the property, stately and imposing and dignified.

Our landlord never so much as lopped off a dead limb or pruned an unyielding branch. The trees had a lonely existence. There was no irrigation system and no sprinklers fed from a pump house to water them. The soil was never weeded or plowed or harrowed or smoothed to receive and hold the water. Yet the trees, watered only by rain, yielded fruit each season.

The problem was what to do with the prunes. They had to be dried out somehow to be real prunes. If they were left on the trees, they grew soft and overripe and dropped on the ground where they were bruised and finally became mushy and rotten and useless.

Of course, as projectiles, they were the size, shape, and weight that you can only dream about. In early stages of growth, the prune is hard and green and rounded and can soar through space with amazing accuracy. A little later in their growth cycle, they soften subtly and splatter squishily on impact. Now and then, I took a bite of a prune, and it had a sharp sweet flavor, but not a taste that I had ever cultivated. Prunes were the neighborhood weapon of choice, and it seemed a waste of time to consume them.

The orchard itself was small, no doubt somebody's family orchard planted years ago. But now I imagined it as my personal grove of trees. If I had been able, I would have cultivated it and nursed it along to new degrees of fruitfulness and then sold the harvested prunes to a cannery. I had many favorites among the trees. They were the ones with handsome trunks rooted firmly in the rich brown soil, with their twisting limbs and branches covered by a hard, dark-brown, cracked, and peeling bark, which clung to the tree like the hide of some prehistoric creature.

The soil in the orchard was the kind you smoothed a little place on and then used little twigs with which to draw your thoughts. I couldn't exactly squat on my hams and draw thoughts like Tom Joad and Jim Casey, but the tip of my crutch served as a writing tool just as well as any twig could. Every once in a while, I wondered what it would be like if all the topsoil were seized by the wind and torn from around the trunks, leaving the roots exposed. The trees would all die and topple over, and then the company tractors would rumble over the property and crush one corner of our house as they plowed everything under. And then Mom and Grandma and I would have to load up the car with a few meager possessions and, along with everyone else, head out to begin a new life in another state. I already knew what books I'd take with me when the time came to leave. And perhaps one day when we camped alongside the road, I'd run into

Abraham and Yetta and share a little stew with them, and Abraham would be so grateful that he'd tell me his life story. The very thought of it made me long for another Great Depression and a devastating dust storm.

We usually had a simple lunch on Saturdays. I left the back porch and entered the kitchen. Mom set a scrambled egg sandwich in front of me.

"Now, take your time eating, Crosby," she said futilely. It was advice I could hardly receive. Sometimes I didn't bother to sit down and eat because eating took me away from my thoughts and always from some exciting plot twist in my books. So I regularly wolfed my food down and fled back to my characters. What interesting lives they had. What tragedies they endured; what obstacles and complications they overcame. Someday I wanted complications like theirs in my life and not like the ones I had, which were dull and boring and uninteresting. Sometimes their unresolved, bittersweet endings seemed preferable to anything in my life. But I wasn't discouraged, for I was in the process of carrying out a foolproof plan of action.

Real life can be a trial when you don't have a plan, and since I am a man of projects and goals, I had long ago dedicated myself to trying to discover the plot of my own life. What were the twists and turns I'd have to experience to achieve my own ending? I had already ruled out an early death, an ending that was too abrupt and left behind too many unanswered questions: for instance, was it worth it? Did I live well? Would anyone miss me? Why didn't I have a father? Where would I be buried? How would Mom and Grandma live without me? What lasting contribution had I made? Who would take care of Beatnik?

Today I followed Mom's advice. I sat down and took a bite out of my sandwich. We couldn't afford real lunch meat. I had scrambled egg sandwiches routinely and never felt ashamed about our lack of cold cuts. I understood what it meant to live on a tight budget and knew that someday we'd get back on our feet and then we'd make up for lost time and I'd have bologna and salami sandwiches every day like everybody else.

Grandma was sitting opposite me. She ate so little that it made me wonder where she got her strength. Just half a sandwich and a gulp of iced tea, and she was done.

Next to me, Mom said, "Crosby, I want you to be on your best behavior tonight." She was always concerned about my aunts and what they'd say and what they'd think of me. Aunt Nelda was the oldest, and she tended to be bossy, always advising Mom on how I should be disciplined. The fact was, I didn't need any discipline. After all, I was the man of the house—with all the rights and privileges thereof. And being disciplined wasn't one of them.

"I'll go to bed early tonight," I said, hoping I wasn't giving away too much. Technically, I always went to bed early, but not exactly to sleep. The back porch was my listening post. I knew where to position myself on the back porch near the kitchen door or at the glass-paneled living room doors so that I didn't miss a word of conversation.

Grandma sipped at her tea and nodded. "I love my daughters, Crosby, but they're not all churchgoers, and sometimes they speak too frankly about their lives, things that a young boy doesn't need to hear." She paused a moment and then said musingly, "I hope Zonell doesn't bring up Arthur Potter."

Mom chuckled and gave Grandma a curious look. "You know that Arthur will be discussed tonight," she said. "Zonell is still in love with him."

"Wasn't he killed in the war?" I asked. Of course I knew this as a fact, having heard the story many times from my listening post on the back porch.

"Yes," Grandma said quietly, "he was killed, and he left behind a brokenhearted girl. Zonell puts too much stock in a man. There were more boys interested in her that you could shake a stick at, and who does she hang on to? The one boy who was killed." Grandma shook her head sadly. "Then what did she do? She married a Lake on the rebound."

For some mysterious reason, Grandma had a low opinion of the Lake family boys, judging them to be a collection of prideful, aloof, redheads. And my Aunt Zonell had committed marriage with one of them. I hoped she would tell the story about Arthur again tonight because she told it with great passion and detail and always wept at the end when she described how he died.

It's hard to resist a good death story, imagining how death must have a cruel personality and come slobbering and shambling after anybody it could. Maybe tonight, Aunt Zonell would add some new details about Arthur Potter's war record.

A Saturday night with my aunts was always a noteworthy event. And the best part was their obligatory summit meeting and gabfest to which I was never invited, but still, as I've pointed out, I always managed to overhear every word. The fact was that few conversations of a private sort could occur at home. I always knew where to post myself. Mom and Grandma had been known to repair behind a closed bedroom door now and then for certain talks, but for the most part, all conversations at home were public domain. I could easily follow a conversation from living room dessert to late night coffee in the kitchen and then back to the living room for more overheard insights and life principles, though many of its juicier tidbits tended to issue forth from a nearly exhausted quartet of sisters.

Aunt Nelda was the oldest. Her husband, Floyd Purcell, was a World War II veteran and hardware salesman. She was very devoted to Floyd's career in hardware sales and had picked up some of his sales jargon. She regularly warned me not to throw a monkey wrench into the works and encouraged me to give a hard sell to every contact. I supposed that some wives heard so much of a husband's trade terminology that it just rubbed off on them. And it happened that Aunt Nelda had two jargon sources to draw from because she had never quite shaken herself free from the influence of her husband's World War II service, and she was apt to say the strangest things.

Uncle Floyd had served in supply depots all over the South Pacific. So Aunt Nelda spoke both military and salesman lingo, sometimes in barbarous combinations. She'd point at me and say, "Crosby, you're my favorite client, so put a hustle on it and be advised that your aunt loves you," or "It behooves the individuals who made this chow to be cited for their service."

Other things she said made even less sense. She called me client most of the time, and once or twice told me to shape up or I'd have to spend the night in the stockade. She arose each morning and saluted a flag she had mounted over her fireplace. The greatest truths in her life were God and country and Floyd Purcell, who rarely visited our home since he was on the road, hustling up new clients, trying out a new sales pitch, or tracking down slippery, unscrupulous clients who owed him money. His sales territory was all over Northern California and Nevada. He drove a baby blue Buick Convertible on which he logged over seventy thousand miles a year. He was stocky and heavy-set. He always wore suits, the trousers of which were secured up over his big stomach, the way Fred Mertz wore his. I once gently suggested to him that he lay his money down for some pants that actually fit him. He just smiled at me and patted his stomach and said that Aunt Nelda's good cooking and his own high living were nothing to be ashamed of.

At about seven that night, Aunt Violet arrived, a cigarette dangling from the corner of her mouth. She smoked so much that when she came to visit, I ordinarily handed her an ashtray at the door.

After a quick puff, she squinted at me and said, "Crosby, don't ever take up smoking. It'll stunt your growth." She wasn't exactly funny, but she tried. She cackled a raspy laugh and patted me on the shoulder as she headed for the kitchen.

The fact was that I had indeed tried smoking. When you have relatives who smoke, acquiring one cigarette is about as difficult as breathing your next breath. Once a pack of cigarettes was within reach on a table, you could extract and palm one and never be noticed. The problem was the taste. Smelling a cigarette being smoked is not the same as smoking one yourself. Mostly cigarettes tasted like ashes, and a single puff always made me dizzy and a little woozy in the head. And I wasn't about to fool with anything that addled my brain or diverted my full attention from stories. A man has to be able to concentrate when he's reading.

I could hear Mom and Grandma greeting Aunt Violet. And a minute later, they were all in the kitchen putting the final touches on a three-layer yellow cake with chocolate frosting.

Aunt Violet was four years younger than my mom and had been married three times. She always spoke with a confident, careless voice about her life and her men and her divorces. She had no hesitation or any qualms about sharing intimate details of her life. She happily wove all the threads of her story into a rather shameless and disturbing tapestry for her scandalized, churchgoing sisters to be properly outraged at.

A few minutes later Aunt Nelda, the oldest sister, arrived with Aunt Zonell, the youngest and most delicate of my aunts. I thought my mom was the prettiest, but the three other sisters had their own points of beauty that I appreciated, though Aunt Zonell had the market on delicate femininity. Mostly, she had an overbite like Dinah Shore. She looked like a movie star.

On the other hand, Aunt Nelda's face was wrinkled and lined and weathered. She never wore makeup, but Aunt Zonell used makeup in ways and proportions that were truly beautifying and left me with a small crush on her. She used something on her cheeks, which highlighted her high, fine cheekbones. That's not to say that Aunt Zonell was perfect, for she preferred heavy red shades of lipstick, which resulted in startlingly accented lips, and a distinct garish red ring around the tip of every cigarette butt. You could track her every move through our home by inspecting ashtrays for her signs. Only Aunt Violet smoked more, but she lacked style. Aunt Zonell was a sophisticated smoker, holding the cigarette carefully in the air between elegant slender fingers and occasionally tapping the cigarette gently on an ashtray so that the ashes never dropped on the floor. But Aunt Violet had an indifferent aim for ashtrays. Whenever she was telling one of her stories and happened at the same time to have a cigarette clinched tightly between her fingers, she tended to gesture wildly with that hand, flinging ashes hither and yon. It was only dumb luck that kept those near her from being covered in a layer of ashes from one of her Lucky Strikes.

By seven thirty we were all in the kitchen, and Aunt Nelda was doing what she did most—bossing us all around and telling us about Uncle Floyd.

"Now, if you people would just follow directions," she began pointedly, "we'd have ourselves a superior time tonight." She was looking directly at my Mom. Of course she meant following her directions and *you people* meant anyone within the sound of her domineering voice.

"There's a way," she continued emphatically, "to conduct such an event so that each individual receives a full ration of fun. Floyd would be in town today, but he's combining business with pleasure in Lodi. It seems a client there is an old army buddy from basic training days. Floyd, of course, served with distinction in the South Pacific." She nodded at us around the table, as though the fact was well known and needed no elaboration.

She went on, "It seems the boy, an individual by the name of Matthew Killian, never rose above the rank of private first class. But he has done an outstanding job in the auto parts business. Floyd is trying to convince Matthew to expand his current enterprise so that it will also include a hardware store in conjunction with the sale of auto parts. I believe Floyd's mission will be successful and that he will achieve his primary objective."

We all agreed that Floyd would make a sale. He was usually so busy that we only saw him from time to time. He and Aunt Nelda lived a simple life. They had no children and lived in a two-bedroom house in Los Gatos. They owned two Buicks—a baby blue convertible for Uncle Floyd, and a black sedan for Aunt Nelda. They treated their cars as though they were their children. Sometimes they cried when one of the Buicks was in the shop for repairs.

"Little Blue has carburetor problems," Uncle Floyd told me once, shaking his head sadly. "And it's all my fault. I drove her too hard, thinking only of myself and not Blue's needs."

Mom asked Aunt Violet how Hamlin Vadney was doing. I had lost track of Aunt Violet's husbands. There was a Ted Terry and a George or Jack Gordon in there somewhere. When she spoke of divorced husbands, Aunt Violet became quite animated, and I had to watch closely or she'd flick ashes on my head with her gestures. I tried to keep an ashtray as close to her as possible, but once she got talking, she became ambidextrous, abruptly switching the cigarette back and forth between hands, and I couldn't place the ashtray fast enough.

Aunt Violet said Hamlin was a pleasant husband, but no real provider. "He's a good man and a hard worker when he stays with it, but he hasn't found himself yet." Uncle Hamlin had been looking for himself since 1947, and his search seemed endless.

"He wants steady work," Aunt Violet said. "But he is so sickly that he misses a lot of days when he should be working, and his bosses always just end up letting him go."

We were all sitting very still and looking at Aunt Violet without comment.

Uncle Hamlin collected money from the government on a regular basis, due to injuries sustained in World War II. He drank a little, but not enough to interfere with him holding down a job. What he did do, and we all knew it, was wander off and forget things. I loved hearing tales about World War II from my uncles or church members I knew who had served, but Uncle Hamlin's story made me shudder. He had a metal plate in his head, surgically placed there as a result of battle wounds received in Sicily. It took Uncle Hamlin two years of recovery and rehabilitation just to get to the point where he could shave and shower himself and remember which was which.

Aunt Violet met Hamlin Vadney a few months after the war ended, when she was waitressing in San Jose at the Pinecone Restaurant. Uncle Hamlin's family lived in Monte Vista, and his sister occasionally took him out to eat in the city. And when she took him to the Pinecone, it was love at first sight for him and Violet. He was making rapid improvements at that time, but after Aunt Violet married him, he plateaued off and stayed there for a while, only to begin losing ground later. He could take care of himself pretty well now and even held down a job sometimes. But occasionally we had to walk through the neighborhood looking for him because he had wandered off again.

Someday, when and if my feet and legs got better, I hoped to serve my country as a soldier, but I didn't want a hubcap-sized hunk of stainless steel inserted under my scalp to go with it.

Uncle Ham and Aunt Violet lived a few blocks away from us on Lomita Street. Aunt Violet still waitressed, as long as she could get someone to sit with Uncle Hamlin in her absence, which was easy to do. Uncle Ham was a calm and gentle soul. His brown eyes were filled with kindness and a certain wondering, quizzical look, as though he wanted to understand the mystery of this thing called existence. He was no strapping specimen of muscular manhood. He was about the same size and weight as Aunt Violet, which was to say medium height and rather light in weight. He liked everyone, and his heart was big. He was one of my best friends.

Once or twice we managed to talk Aunt Violet into bringing Uncle Hamlin to church, but she didn't like our boisterous ways, and so now she only attended during the relatively safe times, such as Christmas or Easter, when Pastor Barker's feet were more or less nailed to the ground and he had to be somewhat formal, if not down-right muzzled. The first time we got Uncle Hamlin in a pew and then requested prayer for him, Pastor bolted out from behind the pulpit like a junkyard dog going after a car thief and, slamming both hands on Uncle Hamlin's head, began to command demons of fear to come out of him.

That was too much for Aunt Violet, who was staring at Pastor Barker as if he were assaulting her husband. After that visit, we couldn't mention church to her without Aunt Violet giving us a blistering account of how she and Uncle Hamlin had been treated.

"I came expecting a peaceful service," she told me one day, "and the next thing I knew, a wild man with a case of the heebie-jeebies was knocking poor Ham around like an old rag doll."

The part about Pastor Barker being a wild man was a fair and astute insight, but I did notice that, right after that, Uncle Hamlin stopped whimpering like a little lost puppy and never resumed the practice.

Mom got up from the table now and began to measure out coffee grounds for ten cups of Maxwell House. All the Plunks regularly stoked themselves up on strong black coffee, and no one made it stronger than Mom. After the proper amount of water was added, she set the coffeepot on the stove and turned the flame up. This was going to be some evening for sure.

Grandma had carefully positioned the chocolate cake in the center of the table. She now began to move around us, placing a fork and plate at each setting. Aunt Violet protested mildly, "Mom, why don't you sit down and let me set the table?" She made as if to rise.

But we all knew better than that. Grandma always waited on her family. "You sit real still, honey," Grandma said, "and I'll take care of everything. There'll be plenty of time for me to sit down later."

Aunt Zonell had come to the house with a paper bag in her possession. The top of the bag was carefully rolled down so that no one could see its contents.

She rose now, paper bag in her arms, and said casually, "I think I'll slip into the living room for a moment. I want to check on something."

When she left the kitchen. I got up and followed her into the other room. Now that we were alone and the kitchen door was shut, Aunt Zonell opened the bag so I could see the treasure inside.

The bag was filled with paperbacks, the kind of books which, according to church standards, I wasn't supposed to read and much less have in my actual possession.

"Crosby," she said hurriedly, "we have to get back in the kitchen because your Grandma is getting ready to cut the cake." She reached in the bag and held up a thick expensive paperback. "Wait till you read this one," she said softly. "The story really crackles, and the characters travel to some very exotic places. You know I have to read my romances and maybe they're not your cup of tea, but this one has a lot of exciting adventure too. Give it a try."

I said I would. "I'll go put these away," I said quietly, taking the bag. We both knew Mom and Grandma should never know exactly what I was reading, but for the last three years, I had been secretly and constantly and zealously reading bag after bag of outlawed paperbacks right under their noses.

Aunt Zonell had begun giving me her old paperbacks on a regular basis when I was confined at home, recovering from the injuries done to my feet and legs. She told me now, "The way I see it, Crosby, is that you can expand your world and your thinking by reading. Now, I know that your Mom and Grandma are big churchgoers and want to protect you from evil, but would you just please take one look at this." And then she reached into the bag I was holding and held up a book, so I could see the cover. "I want you to tell me, Crosby," she said evenly, "where is the evil in this book?"

I looked it over. The price was twenty-five cents, and the cover art was slick and meticulously detailed. It depicted a man in a room lit by a single light bulb, which threw off an ugly blob of yellow light. The man was wearing a rumpled raincoat and a gray fedora hat, and he was bashing an evil-looking thug over the head with a .45, while looking on, crouching in terror in a dark corner, was a terrified young girl.

"Seems harmless to me," I said.

"If you want real evil," Aunt Violet said earnestly, "just read the newspaper. Every day there it is in black and white on your porch—all the evil things people do to each other. Am I right?"

I nodded. Pastor Barker always preached on evil people and evil times. Evil was everywhere. We were given to know that evil was so strong that God could hardly keep things under control and that anyone of us might be suddenly overcome and destroyed by its power. So we better fear and shun all forms of evil in the world. When Pastor Barker preached on the topic, he always included a list of evils to avoid: dancing, worldly music, drinking, parking, all movies, except for *The Ten Commandments*, gambling, immodest dress by women, any random vile women you may encounter, and lastly everything on TV except for religious programs. Other specific evils were added to the list as they came to him and then preached against on Sunday. We had recently heard about a new evil called mixed bathing, meaning a swimming pool shared by everybody, male and female, frolicking in the water together.

But Aunt Zonell, who I never thought of as an evil, bad, or vile woman, had another view: knowledge, she said, should bring power, not fear. And so Aunt Zonell, regarding me as though I were an adult in a child's body, routinely gave me books of all kinds to read.

We had been in the living room several minutes by now, and we needed to complete our book business and get back in the kitchen soon or someone was bound to burst into the room and surprise us with our forbidden literature.

"I'll meet you back in the kitchen," I said. I could go through the curtained, glass-paneled double doors onto the back porch and stash my new paperbacks in the cabinet with the ruined hinges in no time. I had been through this routine many times.

On the back porch, I carefully opened the cabinet and stacked the books prominently among all the others. Sometimes I had to return some books to Aunt Zonell because I didn't want to become too greedy. And besides, I only had limited storage space. But none of that mattered. For once I had read a book, the story and the characters were mine. It didn't matter if I had a copy or not. The characters were now my friends, and any lessons learned on the way just made me stronger and better and wiser.

Back in the kitchen, I gave Mom a pleading look and managed to wheedle a half a cup of coffee out of her to go with the slice of cake I had been served.

She set the cup in front of me. "If this keeps you awake tonight, Crosby, I promise it's the last late night cup of coffee you will ever get from me."

Aunt Nelda would have none of that. "Now, just stand down there, Opal," she said brusquely. "A cup of joe is what all recruits need." Aunt Nelda gave me a fond look, meaning she sort of squinched her eyes up among all the wrinkles lining her face, an expression I had come to recognize as deeply emotional.

Aunt Nelda said to my mother, "Crosby is most definitely officer material, and it is time you and Mom allow this individual to begin the training he needs to achieve promotion."

Evidently, Aunt Nelda saw life as a giant basic training unit. I was a raw recruit with vast untapped potential, and Mom and Grandma were supposed to provide me with the drill I required.

Aunt Nelda said reverently, "Crosby, one day, you may have your own jeep and driver."

Aunt Violet squinted at me through a cloud of cigarette smoke. "If the driver is cute, you could introduce him to me."

Aunt Zonell laughed. "Why, Violet, that wouldn't be appropriate. You're a married woman."

"There's always room for one more good husband," Aunt Violet said lightly, flicking some ashes in my direction.

This kind of talk, getting dangerously close to specifics about husbands and wives, was usually my signal to bow out and retreat to the back porch. But I sat still and let the conversation go on for a few more minutes. Then I began to notice a few warning glances being exchanged between Mom and my aunts, and I knew that if I didn't leave, the course of this conversation would veer off the road, and I would be deprived of the kind of spicy family details that I craved.

I got up a little too quickly. "Well, bedtime for me," I said hastily. "Church tomorrow." I had finished my cake and coffee, and now I made my way around the table, kissing cheeks as I went.

I slipped out of the room and once on the back porch, I posted myself near the kitchen door. Beatnik was lying on my bed. He raised his head and looked at me. He began swishing his tail back and forth, whether as an invitation to pet him or a warning to stay away, I couldn't tell. Either way, I didn't have time for him now.

Meantime in the kitchen, the conversation continued as I'd hoped it would.

Evidently Aunt Zonell had a bone to pick with Aunt Violet. "You talk too carelessly about men," Aunt Zonell was saying. "Not all men are scoundrels and rogues and mere creatures. Some of them can be pretty nice."

Aunt Violet was not offended. "Why, Zonell, what could be nearer the truth? Of course men are creatures. Just like women are. The secret is: never dwell on it. I don't mean it in a bad way. It just gives me a better perspective about marriage: marriage is the union of two creatures. The fact is I've had three creatures for husbands."

I could only imagine the eyes in that kitchen, rolling around in disapproval at Aunt Violet's philosophy. And she wasn't done, for now she went on, detailing the short time she spent with her first husband.

"Ted Terry was sort of my introduction to men as creatures," she said. "He'd show up at our house wearing a Calico shirt and new Levis and cowboy boots, and I'd nearly swoon, he was so handsome. Sometimes we'd laugh right out loud at things he said." She paused and then said rather sadly, "In those days, I was just too young to know what whiskey could do to a man. After I married him and saw he was a mean drunk and a gambler, I just pulled up stakes and left him."

Aunt Zonell sounded concerned. "Didn't your heart break, though? After all, you lived with him for two years and shared a home with him."

Aunt Violet said, "Sharing a home don't make a marriage, Zonell. Ted spent his time drinking, and so I ended up doing the lion's share of work, trying to make us a living." She then said in a musing tone, "I think what I did was fall in love with his clothes. To this day, the very sight of a man in a Calico shirt and a pair of Levis makes me want to go right up to him and ask for a date and then we could marry and have us a real nice honeymoon."

Mom had been silent through all of Aunt Violet's talk. But now she spoke up. "Violet, didn't Georgie Gordon know Ted?" she said a little too quickly.

I was positive that the mention of a honeymoon had provoked the question about George Gordon from Mom. Grandma and Mom, with tact and great skill, were masters at steering conversations away from racy subjects, and honeymoons were chief on the list.

Mom's question worked, for I could hear Aunt Violet's voice turn bitter. "I should have seen that boy for what he was, but there he came, a younger man in love with me, and I was just so flattered at the attention."

There was a pause, and I heard Aunt Violet's Zippo lighter click open and shut. I could almost see the new Lucky Strike dangling from her mouth.

"Ted Terry talked too much," she continued. "Georgie knew I had left Ted, and he thought I was fair game. After a decent amount of time had passed—I think four days had gone by—here he came calling at my door. I hadn't even divorced Ted, and there's Georgie rolling his big blue eyes at me. Well, I couldn't say no to such admiring looks, even if I wasn't completely divorced at the time. And he was so handsome."

Sounding very facetious, Aunt Zonell said, "And how did Georgie look in a Calico shirt and Levis?"

Aunt Violet never missed a beat. "He preferred the lighter colors of Calico. Ted always wore bolder, darker colors." There was a pause. "But I learned my lesson," Aunt Violet said firmly. "Getting divorced was not a habit I ever embraced, but it was thrust on me, and it was the only way to cure my marriages."

Aunt Nelda said, "It was your fraternization with younger troops that brought about your defeat."

Aunt Violet chuckled. "Divorce is no defeat when you can rid yourself of a creature like Georgie Gordon. You see, he was furious about everything, even when he wasn't drinking. He blamed everybody, including God, for all his problems. And on top of that, he told me once that the only reason he married me was because Ted Terry had told him I was frisky. So I knew right away: never marry one of your first husband's drinking chums. It's become a rule with me. I've taken a pledge: don't marry a cute boy who has a previous acquaintance with a former husband. Besides, I don't know where Ted Terry ever got the idea I was frisky."

Grandma said quietly, "I was with your father till the day he died."

Aunt Violet said agreeably, "That's because you're one of the lucky ones, Mom. Lots of women never find the right boy to marry."

"There wasn't any luck to it, Violet," Grandma said sternly. "Your father and I married when we were both seventeen years old, and we just knew we had a lot of work ahead of us to make our marriage work." Her voice softened a little. "We were both born in 1892, and we always thought that was a nice thing to have between us. After all, some people get married with nothing to hold them together."

Mom said, "What was it that attracted you to Daddy?"

"I'd say that your father didn't strike me as a handsome man. He had three brothers, and all the looks in the Plunk family went to them, but your father had a pure heart, and he could laugh louder and longer than any of his brothers. They were all so mournful and serious. You just wanted to cry when you looked at them."

I was now getting genuinely sleepy at my listening post. There was a high degree of tension in what I was doing. I was supposed to be asleep in bed. The thought that the kitchen door would fly open at any moment and I would be caught red-handed eavesdropping made me a little edgy. Still, I remained where I was. This was too good to miss.

"Mom," Aunt Zonell asked, "what made you marry Daddy?"

There was a moment of silence. Then Grandma finally said, "You have to remember the times. I didn't know any other life I wanted. We lived on a farm in Missouri, and all I knew about life I learned from the three or four families near us and the little country church we attended. I wanted a good marriage, and I knew I could make one work. So when Ellis Plunk made his intentions known, I married him."

"How did Daddy make his intentions known?" Mom asked.

"He brought me a dead duck," Grandma said flatly.

I could hear everyone erupt in laughter. I had to back away from the kitchen door so they couldn't hear me laughing. Grandma said the strangest things.

"Boys are real proud of their hunting skills," Grandma explained. "And your father was no exception. When he and his brothers had a particularly good day of hunting, your father would always bring me the plumpest duck. And me, just a girl of fifteen. It only seemed right that he should sit at my family's table and enjoy the fruit of his labors."

"Now, that's a romantic story," Aunt Nelda said firmly. "An individual like our father knew that to advance in this life, he would need the support and loyalty of a proud woman, not one of these squeamish little vain things that hang out at beauty parlors."

My Mom, Aunt Violet, and Aunt Zonell said nothing. They all went to beauty parlors and knew enough not to take Aunt Nelda's bait.

Grandma wasn't through. "Well then, one thing led to another, and before long, my heart just belonged to him."

Aunt Zonell had been silent for several minutes. Now she said quietly, "When Arthur Potter died, I lost my heart."

A silence suddenly hung over the room. I could hear someone sniffling. I judged it was Aunt Zonell and thought she'd turn on the waterworks any second now.

And then suddenly, a chair scraped against the floor, and I nearly jumped out of my skin. I scrunched up behind the door, expecting it to burst open any second. But it didn't. Other chairs then scraped loudly on the floor. I grabbed my crutch and scrambled as quietly as I could over to the bed where Beatnik was lying. He leaped up when he saw me coming, gave me a resentful look and an angry swish of his tail, and then jumped over to his own bed.

I didn't get in my bed. I stood there trying to follow the sounds coming from the kitchen. I figured that the configuration of players was shifting—and that the living room was about to be used for the first time this evening.

If things worked out the way I wanted, Aunt Zonell would be encouraged to continue the story about her lost heart. She was currently married to my Uncle Robert Lake—a quiet, self-effacing man who worked in Cupertino as an accountant at Cali Brothers Feed Store. And it was always puzzling to me that Aunt Zonell could talk about a former love in her life as though she had never recovered from it. What about Uncle Robert? He probably needed at least a smidgen of Aunt Zonell's heart. I had a lot to learn about love.

After a few minutes of hearing the murmuring of voices and the sound of doors opening and closing, I took up a position at a different listening station, this time at the living room doors. I could plainly hear Mom and Aunt Zonell talking.

"You know I love Bobby," Aunt Zonell was saying. "I admit I married him on the rebound. He was Arthur's best friend, and when I found out that my sweet Arthur had died, I needed someone to talk to."

Aunt Zonell was not crying. She was simply explaining the event that had shaped her life and broken her heart.

"Arthur was home on leave when I first met him. He told me all about himself and within a week, I knew I had found a special boy."

Mom said, "He was special. I remember how he treated everybody with such beautiful manners and how he honored you."

I carefully pulled the curtains aside an inch or two—just enough so I could peek into the living room. Aunt Zonell was nodding her head. "He spoke highly of you, Opal. You've always had a way of making people feel at peace. That's why I love coming to your home."

I had to agree with that. Mom and Grandma kept a peaceful home. One of the reasons I could tolerate school and a bully like Clyde Winston was because I knew that no one could invade my home. Grandma told me once, "The devil doesn't dare come knocking on our door. He knows what'll happen if I answer." Grandma always had a glint in her eyes when she talked about the devil.

"When Arthur went overseas," Aunt Zonell was saying, "he wrote me the dearest letters. I learned more about him from his letters than I did when he was here with me. He wrote me letters that were eight pages long, and sometimes longer. He declared his love for me in one of his letters from England and asked me to marry him when he got home. I wrote back that I would. And then his mother called me and told me he had been killed on D-Day. But I didn't believe that for a second. I thought he had been captured and taken prisoner or maybe he'd lost his memory from a wound and was lying somewhere in a hospital recovering and didn't know who he was."

Aunt Zonell dabbed at her eyes with a handkerchief. "After that, I kept receiving letters from him. He was planning out our life together. He said we'd live on a tight budget at first, but because he was a veteran, he would be getting breaks on business loans, and he would get education benefits." She paused and sighed deeply. "I knew that I was receiving letters he'd written just before he died," she explained sadly, "but they were so sweet and real to me. He said that we'd have a place of our own in just a few years. He wanted kids. He said as long as we loved each other the way we did, we could do anything."

By this time, Mom and Aunt Zonell had handkerchiefs flying, wiping, and swabbing at their eyes.

Aunt Zonell dabbed at her eyes again and said miserably, "What makes it so hard is that I have it all in print. I can't bring myself to throw his letters away. When I reread them, I relive every detail."

Mom pointed out delicately, "Bobby Lake is a good and devoted husband to you, Zonell."

"I know that," Aunt Zonell said softly. "He even lets me talk about Arthur. Bobby says he'll love me forever, and he understands what happened and how I feel."

Aunt Zonell sighed and gave my Mom a compassionate look. "I shouldn't talk about this to you, Opal, not after the awful tragedy you and Crosby went through because of Jeff Hoggard and..."

In one fluid movement the curtains dropped out of my hands, and I began to back away from the doors, but I wasn't quick enough to get out of hearing distance, for I clearly heard Mom say, "Jeff was a hard worker, and I felt sorry for him, but it's ancient history and God told me..."

I couldn't hear the rest. I was lying flat on my bed with a pillow over my head. Arthur Potter was one thing, but my father didn't make for a good story—I had formed the habit of never listening to anything about him because Dov and Francie and Neeley and Oliver Twist and Jody Baxter were more interesting, and so were Jim Casey and Huck and Tom and Anne Frank and Horatio Hornblower and the other Jody and his red pony.

After a while I got up and resumed my place at the kitchen door, from which I could easily hear Grandma, Aunt Violet, and Aunt Nelda still talking.

And things were hopping in the kitchen. Aunt Nelda had evidently taken the theme of beauty parlors to its logical conclusion.

"Just suppose the United States was invaded," she said ominously, "the men would be fit to fight because there are veterans out there who haven't lost their appetite for battle. And the women!" she declared sourly, her voice dripping with sarcasm. "The enemy would find them all hair sprayed and bobby pinned, and reading those movie magazines or sitting all high and mighty in those beauty parlor chairs with their heads covered with hair dryers like some kind of space helmet." She paused. "We're soft and complacent, and we've lost our will to fight."

"Just who's going to invade us, Nelda?" Aunt Violet said placatingly. "We didn't get invaded during the war. Why would it happen now?"

Aunt Nelda said, "There is a vast conspiracy always at work to infiltrate and undermine these United States by those dirty Communists." I heard a sudden thump on the table, and then Aunt Nelda said fiercely, "And now we have the possibility of the Pope in Rome telling Americans what to do because we put a Catholic president in the White House."

My head suddenly jerked up. My eyes were opening and closing sleepily, and I was beginning to miss entire sentences. I couldn't stay awake much longer. Besides, tomorrow was Sunday, in many ways the longest day of the week for me. I scooted over to my bed, undressed, and dove under the covers. It was cool enough tonight, with the usual breeze from the Bay, to drop off to sleep easily.

But I kept thinking about my aunts. I hoped Aunt Zonell would be all right. I didn't know how to help her with her broken heart, but it seemed to me you could get over things, given enough time. You could learn new ways to look at scenes from your own life, and then you wouldn't have to be bothered by what anyone else thought about them. But Aunt Zonell held on to the past and let it have power to crush her.

I also wondered why Aunt Nelda was so openly bossy with her sisters, and why her lifestyle was so plain and simple, even severe, when she and Uncle Floyd had plenty of money. And why had Aunt Violet had so many husbands? I loved her dearly, but when it came to marriage, she acted like she was at some bizarre square dance, where the caller, instead of hollering "Change partners!" kept calling "Change husbands!"

My Mom on the other hand was indiscernible. I didn't spend time trying to figure her out. She was simply always there and always hard at work and always my biggest fan. Our home was peaceful because of her confident faith and serene presence. The thought of her remarrying was disturbing and loathsome. Another man in the house was an impossibility. I was fully prepared to despise any suitors. Opal Hoggard was not up for grabs when it came to marriage. Her future was with me.

And I wanted a future, I was thinking sleepily. My aunts had power to shape me, and I loved listening to their stories about the past, and I supposed that when they were younger, they looked ahead to some kind of hopeful and bright future. I wondered how much of what they had dreamed about years ago was in their lives today, for whatever it was, it was shaping me now.

I thought: if you have people around you who speak favorably about life, then you should try to learn from them. Life isn't an explosion of unrelated events that you're stuck with. I had been learning from my aunts that you could become unstuck. They improvised now and then. Like Aunt Violet discarding an odious husband from time to time or Aunt Zonell who was blatantly acting contrary to my church's rules against evil literature by bringing me stacks and stacks of racy books which constantly reaffirmed adventure as one of life's great possibilities.

And perhaps someday, the possibilities I was discovering would yield a satisfying interpretation of the past and show me how to deal with forces which were beyond my control.

The point was that I was constantly learning valuable lessons from my family and my books. Maybe someday I could write all about it. It was actually my number one ambition. I wanted to write. To do so, I needed to keep on listening and reading. But I couldn't help but feel I was missing critically important lessons about life and manhood, seeing as how I was currently always under the influence of women, since my father was dead, and lessons from that direction were gone forever. Not that I'd want them from him even if he were around. I knew that Francie and Neeley had lost their father and that they didn't give up. Their lives advanced. They might have been discouraged, but there was something bigger than the two of them at work.

All at once I had a new thought. Perhaps my plan to become a writer was bigger than me, and it was going to happen no matter what. But I didn't know of any law of inevitability. Something didn't sound right. Mostly I thought I had a lot of work ahead of me if I really wanted to write.

I closed my eyes and pulled the blankets up under my chin. Maybe I was concentrating too much on these things. My head was swimming. Over on his bed, Beatnik was curled up in a ball, sleeping quite soundly. I doubted if he had any thoughts swirling around his furry cat head.

And before I knew it, sleep took me, and I only dreamed one dream. I was arguing with Clyde Winston. We were at school surrounded by classmates, and Clyde was threatening me. I told him if he took another step toward me, I was going to swing my crutch at him and slice his fat face open. Clyde took another step, and I started crying because I didn't want to hurt him. I just wanted him to like me. I didn't hate him, but it seemed like he knew something about me that made me detestable, and I didn't know what that something was. More evidence that I was missing important lessons somehow. The dream lurched to a halt, and Clyde never reached me.

After that, I didn't dream anymore.

* * * * *

-SUNDAY-

Sundays were cast in stone. We had a rigid routine set for the day that we followed meticulously or we would never survive the rigors of a typical Sunday with its emotional depths and heights.

The first order of business was our clothing, which Mom and Grandma attended to, sometimes days in advance because there wasn't time for an extra blink of an eye on Sunday mornings. Our afternoon meal, the biggest of the week, was tended to next. Food preparation on Sundays had a touch of danger to it, for after sliding a pan with that week's tasty cut of meat onto the oven rack, Mom would shut the oven door and then run the risk of leaving the oven on while we went to church. But it was a risk worth taking—Sunday afternoon meals made up for a lot of things.

It used to be when I was wearing leg braces, Mom would massage my leg muscles each morning, hoping it would prepare me for a more comfortable day. She thought it helped, and I didn't discourage her. In those days, nothing helped my legs and feet feel better. But I had come a long way since then, and yet I was reluctant to simply discard the one crutch I was still using. In some strange way, I was dependent on it, even though my feet had straightened out and my legs were feeling stronger every day.

Walking without crutches had been ruled out of my life by our family physician, Doctor Walters. He had been adamant about it, but Grandma said God hadn't ruled out any such thing. She often told me that God could do anything he wanted to. So one day, I asked her if that was true, why didn't God give us a home of our own and give Mom a better job and give me a father.

On that occasion I made both Mom and Grandma grab their handkerchiefs. Some subjects were very sensitive to them, I realized. But I was the realist, and no subject repelled me. I could talk about most anything. And because I was a man of letters, I had to be open-minded and a little world weary and somewhat brooding and always prepared to discuss life's darkest secrets, just like in my books where the characters never ran out of clever and barbed words with which they discussed their complicated, embattled, and bitter lives.

Sadly, our Sunday morning routine never left me time to read. So after I dressed in freshly ironed black trousers and a white shirt, I tied a neat half Windsor knot in the thin black tie around my neck and then presented myself to Mom and Grandma for inspection.

They looked me over and then Mom said, "I'm glad Brother Maston taught you how to tie a tie, Crosby, because you look so handsome: like a young Jimmy Stewart."

I admit I rather enjoyed the compliment. "Thank you for the nice words," I said sweetly. "At least you didn't tell me I look like a young Jimmy Durante."

After that, the three of us arrayed in our Sunday best, walked the short distance to the church.

Our Sunday morning routine wasn't the only thing cast in stone. By comparison, church customs were firmly set, institution-alized and made of granite—a real fortress of tradition. I'll never understand the reason, but Sunday school began at nine forty-five sharp. Never did it start fifteen minutes sooner or half an hour later. There was something rigid about all of it.

And my place rain or shine at nine forty-five was in the Sunday school classroom up in the church loft. The church had a peaked roof, which left space for an upstairs loft with its slanted ceiling and one small window. The space had been converted into a small Sunday school room, sloping ceiling and all. I had to be careful how I backed my chair up in that room or I'd bang my head against the ceiling.

I was in the Junior boys class. Our Sunday school teacher was Brother Maston. He was about twenty-five years old and worked as a carpenter. He wore his black hair swept back pompadour-style with lots of pomade to hold it in place. He looked like a hood, but he was kind and outgoing and well liked by all the Junior boys because we could get him off the subject and onto something more interesting in no time at all. While the other Sunday school classes were being instructed in the life of Moses or Jacob or the Martyr Stephen, the Junior boys were discussing how the tabernacle in the wilderness might be built today if you had an air compressor and one of those new fangled nail guns. All of us Junior boys hoped to grow up someday and have our very own sixteen-penny nail gun. Brother Maston told us the secret of how to hold up the safety guard with one hand and then shoot sixteen-penny nails at sheetrock. We also talked about the many battles the Hebrew people fought and how one bazooka or one M4 Sherman tank would have turned the tide of battle. And one memorable Sunday morning, we considered the young shepherd boy, David. We asked ourselves, wouldn't a Thompson submachine gun have been much more efficient than a simple slingshot against Goliath? Either way, we concluded, Goliath never had a chance.

Brother Maston was a great Sunday school teacher. Most of us boys wanted him to pastor the church—he was that good at teaching the Bible.

There was an interval of about ten minutes between Sunday school and the morning worship service. In that time, the choir got robed and took its place up front while the children and adults found their seats in the main sanctuary. The pews were a series of rather uncomfortable folding wooden seats, varnished an indifferent dark brown, and arranged in rows that were a little too close together.

Once everyone was seated, the formal morning worship service began. We sang two hymns, and then it was time to raise your hand and state your prayer requests. Brother Santiago was first. He always asked that we pray for rain. It didn't matter what time of year it was, or how it looked outside, he never failed to remind the church of the need for more rain.

Next, Sister Fitts—a tall, bulky woman—was recognized. I nearly groaned out loud. We were in for it now, I was thinking. Sister Fitts had her usual long string of indelicate requests, beginning with her oldest son, Patch. He was a worthless boy, a rebel, a secret smoker, a car thief, and a juvenile delinquent, according to his mother. She said, "He's on his way to jail if God don't interfere." I was sure she meant if God didn't "intervene," but I suspected that if I pointed out the verbal slip to her, she'd probably request prayer next Sunday for Crosby Hoggard, who was such a mean and disrespectful young man. So I let it pass.

The next on the list was her daughter, Rose, who Sister Fitts said was running around with the wrong crowd and was probably going to sin a terrible sin and bring shame to her family because she didn't know anything about the birds and the bees or babies or anything else. Finally, Sister Fitts asked that we pray for her shiftless, so-called husband, Chuckie, that he act more like a man and take his place as the head of his family.

Standing next to her, Chuckie said, "Amen" to that request. Patch and Rose, on her other side, remained quiet and kept their heads bowed.

There were many other requests: for a sick child, a backslidden husband, a broken-down car, money to pay bills, a job, for bigger crowds on Sunday. And there were several "unspoken" requests— some things were too delicate to mention out loud to the congregation. I couldn't help but notice that Sister Fitts had no unspoken requests.

What followed then was a loud season of prayer that could be heard five blocks away. It sounded like an unruly mob preparing themselves to storm an enemy's castle, but first they had to lash themselves into a shrieking frenzy. Thankfully, a few minutes later, one of the church elders, Brother Fogerty, stepped up to the pulpit and concluded the morning prayer time in a slightly lower voice, which is to say you could only hear him two blocks away.

After prayer, Pastor Barker strode forward and placed his pudgy hands on either side of the pulpit.

Pastor J. Willie Barker was short and round with several rolls of flesh erupting out of his shirt collar. It was well known that any visit from Pastor Barker nearly emptied out a refrigerator. His head was bald down the middle with hair on the sides, which he wore long and swept up and over his shiny scalp. Combed thusly, his hair had the appearance of a poorly matted rag rug. Sometimes the two sweeps of hair met in the middle and didn't lie down flat, which I don't think was his intention. The hair formed a ridge that ran from just above his brow to just below his shirt collar. It was an embankment, sometimes rather peaked and other times quite flattened. Grandma loved the man and his ministry, but his hair deformities made her want to switch churches. Several small children had told me they never got near him for fear that his hair might rise and walk. I once considered making a request at prayer time for Pastor's hair transgressions, but I couldn't do it with a pure heart.

Pastor Barker's sermons gave me many hours of thinking pleasure. I could almost smell the tropical flowers under the hot Hawaiian sun, and I could almost see Abner Hale preaching to the natives in Hawaii. I sometimes smiled with great satisfaction, for I could almost feel the soil of the reclaimed land in Palestine sifting between my fingers. I positively glowed at the thought of planting dozens of Australian Eucalyptus trees around the swampy, malarial ground and how I would wait patiently for the swamps to dry up. And then the planting would begin, and the earth would yield up a bumper crop of grapes or dates or figs or citrus fruit in no time at all.

However, there was an unusual consequence to the thoughts I had in church. My face was evidently rather innocently transparent when I was thinking, and Pastor, noticing my yearning, intense, and joyful expression, apparently misunderstood its cause and jumped to the conclusion that his sermon was really getting to me. It truly inspired him. He'd preach like a windmill at that point, his pudgy arms energetically whirling around and around, his voice rising in pitch, and his chubby cheeks getting redder and redder. I could only hold my breath for thirty seconds, but Pastor could begin a sentence, go off on a tangent, and get back on track without so much as one gasp for air. I timed him once at fifty-five seconds. I don't remember what he was saying, but I do recall how he said it with one long breath-holding crimson-faced display.

This Sunday morning meant a lot to Grandma. She thought so highly of Dad Upland that out of respect for him, she'd worn a hat to church. It was a plain straw hat with a wide brim and three faded red plastic flowers on the side. Grandma only wore it on special occasions, and I'd noticed this morning that she had marched to church with a certain formal dignity, even a little pomp. Wearing the straw hat always produced an elegant effect in her manner.

I always sat near the front in one particular pew on the left side of the auditorium. From there I could comfortably hear every single note of Sister Barker's organ music. Her nimble fingers always flew expertly across the keyboard, and by the time we had sung two hymns and had completed prayer time, she already had one shoe off. She was so small compared to her husband that I often wondered if a mistake had been made by the Almighty in putting the two of them together. But then again, perhaps when the Almighty put them together, Pastor Barker had been as thin as a rail, and then later in their married life, it turned out his wife was a sensational cook, and she'd fattened him up by serving him too many tasty dishes. But no matter how you sliced it, they didn't match in size, shape, or form.

Besides the church organist, I had another reason for sitting on the left side of the church. It was to avoid the right rear pews where the young mothers sat with their hungry infants. It was unsettling enough to know what was going on back there, but it was even worse hearing babies slurping noisily away while Pastor Barker preached. Sometimes those young mothers gave their babies the Gussie all service long. It was all I could do to keep my eyes off them and on Sister Barker's dainty little feet where they belonged.

With his hands clutching both sides of the pulpit, Pastor Barker now led the church in one more hymn. Then he made a few announcements. My favorite announcement this morning came after Pastor Barker had glanced quickly at the right rear pews in the auditorium. He then said rather solemnly, "For any of you young mothers who have infants and don't know it, we have a lovely nursery in the back of the church." I puzzled over that one for several minutes.

Pastor went on. He said that this morning's offering would be taken after our guest speaker delivered his message.

Then he introduced Sister Joyce Raedena Eardley, who was going to sing what Pastor termed a "special number." It certainly was special, all right. If there was a relationship between the key the song was played in and the melody it was sung in, it escaped me. The song seemed uncommonly long, but finally, Sister Joyce warbled on up to a high tremulous climactic note that brought tears to all the eyes around me and to mine also, though, I judged for a different reason.

I had sat through many of Sister Joyce's specials. This one was made somewhat more bearable because while she was singing, the door up front on one side of the platform opened, and Dad Upland came out. He moved rather shakily to one of the high-backed chairs behind the pulpit and sat down. He wasn't paying much attention to the preliminaries. His hair was stark white, and he had a mad tangle of stiff white hair for eyebrows. He was wearing a very neat two-piece gray suit and a white shirt with a frayed collar and adorning his ensemble was the standard thin black tie. His shoes were highly polished, and when he crossed his old skinny legs and one foot came up a little, you could see holes in the soles of his shoes. He had his Bible opened on his lap. Regardless of his clothing, he had an ambassadorial dignity and an imposing presence.

After Sister Joyce had finished her special song and had left the platform to sit down among the congregation, Pastor Barker once again stepped up to the pulpit. "Our guest speaker this morning needs no introduction," he said with a huge smile. "He was last here some three years ago, as many of you will well remember."

He paused and looked over the congregation. It seemed to me that his passing gaze settled directly on Mom and Grandma and me. Mom and Grandma were sitting very still and looking steadily back at Pastor Barker. I wondered briefly why I didn't remember Dad Upland.

Pastor resumed his introduction. "Dad will not only be speaking this morning, but we are also praying that God will open the door for him to address us this evening. But right now, I want to invite Reverend Garland 'Dad' Upland to deliver the word to us."

And then deliberately and with some difficulty, Dad Upland made his way to the pulpit.

"Oh, he's slowed down so much," I heard someone whisper from the other side of the auditorium.

He looked tired. He held both sides of the pulpit, not so much as a preaching stance, it appeared to me, but more to hold himself up. His voice was steady and calm.

"It don't seem right that my darling wife, Hulga Mae, died so young," he said. "But the Lord needed her in Heaven and took her home. And it doesn't make sense that my boy, Merle, got the consumption and coughed up blood every night on his pillow for a year. He just wasted away. But I wanted him to live."

Now, this was a sermon I could listen to. I like a well-told death story. A real good tale about death should have a meaning and a moral. It should be like Jim Casey's death, who died so noble; or Fodder-wing who named Jody Baxter's fawn before he died.

Dad's voice was soft, but emphatic as he continued. "If there was no Heaven, I'd have to give up because of the pain in my heart. But I can't complain because I'm going there soon."

And to make his point, he abruptly slumped over the pulpit. I thought it was a good illustration of the nearness of death. But at the same instant that Dad had collapsed, Pastor Barker, for all his bulky size, had instantly leaped to his feet and was behind Dad, gently supporting him in his arms.

A general state of confusion followed. I thought Dad was being dramatic when he slumped over, but it looked like he was having a heart attack or a stroke right up there in front of the whole church.

Pastor was holding him and lowering him gently to the platform floor. From where I was sitting, I could see Dad's feet sticking out from behind one side of the pulpit and his snow-white hair on the other. I noticed Brother Maston running out the side door, and I judged he was running to the nearest phone so he could call an ambulance.

Several of the more hysterical types of the congregation were praying as loud as they knew how for God to do something. Chief among them was Grandma. Then, at about the time when things couldn't have become more loud and disorderly, one of Dad's feet gave a healthy jerk. Everyone was trying to get their two cents in. "Don't move him!" someone yelled. "Move back and give him some air!" another shouted. Then someone wailed, "It's his home going time!" Someone else screamed, "Give him some water!"

I thought they were all going mad. Then I saw his other foot give a jerk, and a wave of relief washed over me. Maybe he'd just blacked out for a second and he was going to be all right and the crisis would pass. And then if he got up off the floor and finished his sermon, everyone would simmer down. He hadn't made any major points yet about death, but he'd sparked my imagination, for just before he collapsed, I was putting together a short survey of characters from my books who had died and what their deaths meant.

I wasn't the only one who had seen Dad's feet move. Others had noticed, and now two church elders were helping him to his feet, which caused the hysterical types to go from bad to worse. They began to thank God for a miracle. They were shouting and dancing and pounding each other on the back. The problem was that when you expected the worse and there was then some sort of change from worse to less worse, then that was a miracle to some people.

I was getting more and more disgusted. I decided to go outside and wait on the church steps. I looked back when I got to the church doors. Dad was sitting up, brushing off his suit, a sheepish grin on his face.

Out in the daylight, I sat on the steps and assessed the situation going on inside the building. Hopefully, Dad was now on his feet, ready to complete his sermon. Once done, he should leave town as fast as possible. The whole thing was probably just a brief fainting spell. Perhaps he was a constitutional inadequate, susceptible to maladies of all sorts, and this type of collapse was a usual thing in his preaching. Or maybe he'd staged the whole thing, and it was some sort of plot to take over the church. Then the whole community.

I was really enjoying this train of thought, when I looked around at a commotion behind me, and there was Grandma Plunk, hat askew, coming out of the church arm in arm with Dad Upland.

He had a handkerchief the size of a tablecloth in one hand raised over his head, waving it around like he was signaling a ship at sea. I had to move over on the steps to let Dad and Grandma through. Behind them came Pastor Barker and the rest of the congregation, waving more handkerchiefs and looking like they were going to burn down everything in their path as they marched across Georgia with General Sherman.

It was the simple truth that our church was known for its eccentricities. I didn't follow all of their practices. I was very individualistic, and I made up my own mind on church practices. For instance, on occasion when everybody else was shouting the victory, I'd shout and holler a little too. Mainly I was yelling at everybody else to be quiet and stop interrupting my thoughts, but with them hollering so loud, my words and sentiments were completely drowned out.

And now to my astonishment, the handkerchief brigade began to march off down the street, where they turned left on Pasadena Avenue. They apparently were parading around the block! My exasperation was reaching new heights. I got up and walked to my right and stood there on the corner as though I were chiseled in stone, staring up Orange Avenue past our house to Steven's Creek Boulevard. The neighbors were going to call the police or the riot squad if these people didn't calm down.

From where I was standing, I could easily see the other end of the street, and when, several minutes later, I saw the first few marchers coming around the corner, I began to feel like it wasn't so bad after all. They'd all be back here soon, filing timidly back to their seats, where perhaps they might even return to whatever senses they still had.

But I was somewhat premature in my optimism, because the mob suddenly seemed to be slowing down and not coming immediately back to the church.

In fact, they had halted at my house and were now flooding through the gate and standing in the front yard. I headed for home and pushed through the crowd, only to discover Dad Upland standing on our front steps, addressing the troops.

Dad didn't look tired now. His voice rang out. "The devil can't kill me so easy," he said with that certain glint in his eye, the same one that Grandma always displayed when she mentioned the enemy. "I'm going to keep on living, because the Lord has shown me that I still have several tasks ahead of me. I want to finish my course with joy and fight the good fight of faith to the end. I don't know exactly the time of my home going, but I'm confident the Lord does."

The people were smiling and amening every word. "Years and years ago," Dad went on, "the Lord brought my darling Hulga Mae across my path in Los Banos, California. She was a simple farm girl, and I knew when I first saw her that she'd be my wife. It broke my heart when she left me and went home to glory."

The crowd now had a practical use for all those handkerchiefs. They were swabbing away at their eyes. I was wondering why the old coot was preaching at my house, on my front steps, and telling us about his love life. He was over eighty years old for Pete's sake.

Dad went on, "Now that my darling Hulga Mae is gone, the Lord has brought a new someone to me." Suddenly, a chill like a bad fever brings gripped my body. I began to shiver like a wet dog under the porch on a freezing winter day.

Of course, Dad now told the crowd who that new someone was. "The lovely Bessie Ida Plunk has agreed to marry me." He announced it like they'd had months and months to consider the pros and cons of getting married instead of the seven or eight minutes they'd had to march around the block.

Everyone cheered the announcement. My mother and grandmother were both standing on the steps near Dad. He extended his hand to my Grandma, and she proudly stood, straw hat slightly askew, next to Dad.

I wanted to start the day over. If I could travel back through time to this morning, I'd have Grandma stay home with me. I'd claim that my legs hurt. Time travel was theoretically possible, according to Einstein, and definitely possible in H. G. Wells. But I was here in California on Orange Avenue, standing in my own front yard on a Sunday morning. I agreed with FDR: this was a day that would live in infamy. Dad Upland had suddenly and deliberately attacked my peace of mind.

After Grandma went up on the porch and stood with Dad, things began to calm down a bit, and then a few minutes later, the crowd began to make its way back to the church for I don't know what, because I couldn't take any more surprises, so I stayed home. I'd seen and heard enough.

I am nothing if not logical. Thinking through thorny problems, considering creative possibilities, and formulating inspired alternatives were my stock in trade. I had been prepared for life's eventualities by the many ideas and solutions I'd found in my reading. And right now, I needed a place to sit and think and plan.

Our house was one of the best in the neighborhood, at least to me. And it always seemed to me that we'd never be able to make the monthly rental payment. Seventy dollars was a lot of money. I worried about two things: paying the rent, and more specifically, paying the rent on time. School harassed me a few hours a day, five days a week, but the inability to make rental payments on time—and the thought of losing our home—left my heart pounding with fear.

In the first place, I thought the owner of the house, the nervous, unsmiling Mr. Trumball—a man I never looked at directly when he came to collect the rent—felt sorry for us and had let us have the place out of pity. He probably knew that Mom and Grandma were widows, and so, out of some guilty sense of compassion, he grudgingly let us live at the big house on Orange Avenue for what he must have thought was a low rent. But rent was always an issue. So far, Mom had diligently scraped enough money together each month to make the payment on time.

I was well acquainted with fine houses and gracious living, because I'd seen Wally and Beaver's home. The Cleaver family never worried about rent. From what I could observe, the Cleavers owned their home, an achievement that I knew must have made them very happy. As for me, I never wanted to move from here, and I'd often wondered how to go about buying the place, which was probably an impossibility.

By now, the last of the handkerchief brigade had disappeared around the corner of Orange and Granada. They were all back inside the church. I had no desire to join them.

I went in the house and closed the front door behind me. I leaned against it for a moment. It was time for me to consider a few possibilities. I then headed for the back porch.

Beatnik was curled up on his bed and never gave me a glance. I sat in the middle of my bed and thought about the fetid, over-powering stench of unwashed bodies at Andersonville prison. Then I walked a path of hard-packed earth, leading from my cabin in Florida for a full half mile, so I could bring home two buckets of water from the pool there and then later Jody Baxter and I would play with our pet deer named Flag. I could almost feel my well-concealed .45 resting snugly in my shoulder holster, a fedora hat sitting rakishly on my head, and there she was: a gorgeous secretary bringing me a mug of joe. But then reality set in.

My thoughts now focused on Dad Upland and Grandma and Mom and me. If a marriage was about to take place, just exactly where were the newlyweds going to live? Here on Orange Avenue? I didn't want any intruders. This house belonged to me. Suddenly school didn't seem so bad a place, and Clyde Winston was a close and very dear friend of mine. I had the grim feeling in my guts that Dad was going to move in with us. That would mean anarchy in my kingdom.

I would have to lead a revolution that would make Fidel Castro look like one of the Marx Brothers by comparison. I could wall off the back porch as my Warsaw Ghetto. I would slip out at night through the sewers and make a run for food and ammunition. Another man in the home meant competition for attention and a division of affections. Mostly it meant a change in my realm of dominion. I would not give up easily.

So sitting there, with the sun's rays striking me warmly in the face, I began to make a plan, but the sun annoyingly got to me, and I curled up like Beatnik and was asleep in no time.

When I woke up, Grandma was calling me to supper. We ate hugely on Sunday afternoons. Pastor Barker knew that church had to end by twelve o'clock on Sunday mornings or every pot roast in the congregation would burn to a crisp. During Pastor's sermon on Sundays, you could see dozens of wives darting furtive little glances at the clock. And since Pastor regularly ate at someone's home on Sundays, he tended to be prompt, if not downright exact, in delivering a rather abrupt benediction at the stroke of noon.

I came through the kitchen door and there, as I should have anticipated, was Dad Upland sitting at the table with Mom and Grandma. They were all staring at me. They didn't seem to be tense, but they were looking at me expectantly. I must have slept for over an hour. The table was set, and Mom and Grandma were still dressed in their Sunday best. I decided to play along and try to figure out what Dad was up to.

Mom said grandly, "Crosby, we have a special guest to join us for our meal." Grandma looked shyly at me.

Dad was older up close. Those spiky, stiff white eyebrows were frowning at me like another set of eyes. He had wrinkles on top of wrinkles. He was very thin and was still wearing the suit he had preached in. His pale blue eyes shone like light bulbs.

"I'm glad to meet you, Brother Upland," I said genially. There was no use in giving away too much of my interior life. I may have been rather agitated by this intrusion, but all I showed was simple good manners and a subdued and decorous outward behavior.

And part of those good manners was to refrain from telling Dad that he was sitting in my place and that in this kingdom I held the ruler's scepter which I hadn't extended to him.

"And it's nice to see you again, young man," Dad said kindly. Grandma and Mom shot Dad a warning glance, or so it appeared to me. They were genuinely alarmed at Dad's comment. It seemed like a harmless greeting to me, and besides, the table was running over with heaps of luscious food, and I was too hungry to think about Dad's words.

Our table held a juicy pot roast tied neatly with string arranged around it in a series of circles. It was my job to cut the strings and carve the meat. There was a bowl of steaming green beans, which had been simmered in their own juices with chopped-up pieces of bacon added for flavoring. Another bowl was filled with mounds of fluffy mashed potatoes, made with gobs of butter and canned milk. One platter held corn on the cob from Grandma's own garden. Sitting in the center of the table was a gravy boat, filled with a thick golden-brown gravy made from the meat drippings. It was prepared especially for me, since I always dowsed my food with a generous layer of gravy, corn on the cob included. I freely admitted it was a messy habit, but the benefits outweighed the sticky fingers. We had a special oversized salad bowl filled with shredded leaf lettuce, sliced radishes, avocados, cucumbers, carrots, and tomatoes. I usually ate two helpings of salad, drenched in Mom's concoction of oil and red wine vinegar.

Mom asked Dad Upland if he would be so kind as to say the blessing over the food. Dad's soft voice intoned, "Father, you saved this dear young boy's life for a reason and I'm glad I was there and I'm still around to see him." I heard a distinct thumping sound coming from under the table, not a very loud sound, but still noticeably, someone got kicked. Dad went on, "Now bless this food and strengthen our bodies to serve you." We all amened.

When I opened my eyes and looked around, I could see that Mom was plainly uncomfortable. Grandma at once began passing bowls of food around the table.

I realized I wasn't picking up the signals. Why wasn't Mom looking at me? Why had Dad said it was nice to see me again? Did he mean see me again since this morning in church? And who got kicked under the table?

If all that food hadn't been in front of me, I probably would have pursued some answers. But right now, the thing to do was to dig in.

Dad filled his plate too modestly for me. I could live on mashed potatoes and gravy, but Mom always said I needed vegetables too. So, in keeping with Mom's injunction, I dished out a few green beans on my plate. I spaced them carefully so that no two of them crossed each other. The appearance was both pleasing and yet mildly deceiving to the eye: I truly had a portion of vegetables in obedience to Mom's advice, but not enough in number to outrage my palate. Both the spirit and letter of the law had been upheld.

When the gravy boat was finally passed my way, I gently poured a liberal coating over everything on my plate. And amazingly, by that time, Dad had one or two bites left to eat.

"So, how long have you been preaching?" I asked Dad pleasantly.

He wiped his mouth and said, "I was called to preach the Gospel when I was twelve years of age. I had been running from God for many years up to that time, but one day in the summer of 1887, I was working in the pasture of my Uncle Orvil's place in Broken Arrow—when suddenly an awful sense of conviction hit me. I had never known a feeling like that in my life. I began to call on God to set me free and break the chains of darkness that were holding me."

Dad went on. I had hit upon a familiar theme, and Dad's voice had easily fallen into the groove of the story. I imagined him telling this story over the years in countless churches, using these exact words. He told the story dispassionately, as though it had all happened to someone else. It seemed to me that when you're eighty-five years old, you really are talking about someone else who is long gone.

He was saying things that were hard to believe. He said he had been healed of goiter, whatever that was, and after that, anyone he prayed for with a goiter condition was instantly healed. He described times and places I couldn't comprehend. He spoke of preaching for weeks in some churches and making only pennies or nothing at all. Evidently, grinding poverty was all he'd ever known.

He covered his life and ministry up to and including World War I. When no one at the table said anything, he went on to the roaring twenties and the Great Depression. He was always moving around and always preaching. The names of the places he passed through were musical; Bugle, Texas; Flurry, Iowa; Liar's Heaven, Oregon; San Martijo, California; Blue Mustang, Oklahoma; Stinkblister, Missouri; Hanging Noose, Wyoming. And from each place issued a story, succinct and absorbing and miraculous, telling about God's work in each location.

Grandma and Mom were listening to all of this rather sedately, but I was growing a little weary of so many details.

At one point, he paused for a breath, and I jumped in and asked him, "Have you ever seen anybody die?"

Mom glared at me, giving me one of those looks that said, *You're going to hear about this later!* Grandma made little fluttering movements with her hands, an apologetic expression on her face.

But Dad never hesitated. "I've been at the bedside of many a dying saint and sinner and watched death win its squalid and ignoble victory." He shook his head sadly. "I've seen death take a widow's beloved son away. I've wept till I couldn't weep anymore."

Dad was waxing eloquent and painting vivid word pictures. I'd often wondered what death smelled like, and I'd marveled at just how close people are to death. Basically, the human predicament is that you don't know from one breath to the next when death will take you. Abraham Lincoln didn't know, or he never would have gone to Ford's Theater, and all it took was one bullet.

And for that matter, I wondered how many one-bullet tales of death could be chronicled. And what about Harry Houdini taking one punch in the stomach? And there was always Pearl Harbor and Kamikaze pilots and the ovens of Auschwitz and FDR felled by a cerebral hemorrhage and one atomic bomb dropped on Hiroshima.

Suicide was an aberration, man playing God, trying to beat death to the finish line. I often wondered why a good, loving, and strong God would allow so much cruel death to cover the earth. And if he was so good, why didn't he just take over, do away with death, and make everything right? And of course, on the other hand, if the devil was so strong and evil, why didn't he take over and make everything wrong? There seemed to be a conundrum here: a contest was in progress every day, but most of the rules of play were hidden from me.

Job proved a contest existed. I gathered that God had a lot of confidence in Job's ability to hang on even when the devil was permitted by God himself to do anything he wanted to do to Job, short of killing him outright.

I had the habit of begging God to please don't make me another Job. One was enough. I'd never read the book of Job; I'd only heard about him in sermons, and the thought of reading the entire story in the Bible filled me with dread. What if I read it and discovered things about God that were best left undiscovered? What if God really did organize contests with the devil, and he had me on today's schedule with an asterisk by my name, designating Crosby Hoggard as the current MVP?

My dread of the book of Job boiled down to a reading problem. I realized that when I was reading words in my books, some kind of strange alchemy was going on. I was looking at ink on paper, arranged according to certain rules of grammar and syntax into recognizable symbols, which I had learned how to unscramble. But every reading moment seemed so real to me, that the next thing I knew, I was always swept up and taken captive by the force of the narrative. Then I was plopped down in the center of the story, fully living it, which was precisely why I never read Job: I didn't want to be in the center of that story! I always skipped from the book of Esther, right past Job, and went directly to the Psalms.

Now, though, there was no use stating any of this around the table. Dad was finished with his stories about death and had moved on, pursuing the events of his life up through World War II. It was always the same: traveling, preaching, and praying, followed not surprisingly by another plunging degree of grinding poverty.

It had been arranged that Dad would spend the afternoon with Brother Maston. The church would frown on a single male napping at the home of two widows. A meal in the company of two women was perfectly acceptable, but church polity and practice dictated that Dad had to go elsewhere for an afternoon siesta.

It was just as well that he left our home. I had some more thinking to do. I was beginning to wonder why Dad Upland seemed a bit familiar to me. This morning, Pastor Barker had said that Dad was at our church three years ago, but I had no memory of that visit. Right now I wanted to be alone so I could ponder the subject on my mind: the rather shadowy Dad Upland.

I excused myself from the table and once again went out on the back porch to my thinking place. I didn't go empty-handed. Beatnik's bowl was in a corner of the kitchen floor. I wasn't the only one who craved mashed potatoes and gravy.

On the back porch, Beatnik nearly climbed my leg to get to his food. I set it down, and as cats do, he began to eat rather daintily.

I sat on my bed and tried to reason out my preoccupation with Dad Upland. For one thing, he was about to upset the balance of my personal life and comfort. Granted he was interesting in a certain eccentric way, like a strange new specimen under a microscope. But why didn't I remember his visit three years ago?

Beatnik—done eating, leaped up on the bed and sat on my lap, nudging my hand. I began to scratch behind his ragged orange ears, and he looked dreamily up at me. Life was simple for a cat, I thought, but not so simple for me.

So I began to break things down into their component parts. Dad was a puzzle to me. He seemed adjusted and undisturbed about his life. He was poor, somewhat bedraggled in overall appearance, rather shabbily dressed, and needed widows to feed him, but he had dignity and composure. He was peaceful and had seemingly small ambitions, whereas I had lofty ambitions. Mom was always telling me to calm down, take it easy, and rest. Even on crutches, I moved around like a whirling top and rarely had a moment of peace. My agitated brain sometimes conducted imagined arguments with teachers and preachers and playground bullies, disputes that were heated and angry and intense. I mostly won those arguments because of my clever and cutting wit, leaving me with a deep, satisfied feeling.

But then again, my thought life had a peculiar physical effect on me: my own thoughts sometimes caused me to turn blood red in the face from embarrassment and shame at what I was thinking. Why was it that by myself—just me and my thoughts—my face would sometimes flame with redness? I wondered if Dad's face ever turned red because of what he was thinking.

Not that I was abnormal in the thinking department, but I was rather uneasy about my seeming lack of control. My ambition to be a writer meant that I needed to cultivate a rigorous and well-disciplined pattern of thought, deliberately brought about by my extensive reading, but I didn't need to embarrass myself in the process.

Probably Dad Upland hadn't read anything of merit in his life. At dinner, he never once quoted the great names of literature, like Hemingway or Steinbeck or Wolfe or Zane Grey. Instead, Dad had used places he visited and people he knew to extract meanings and interpretations. I admitted that Dad gave the appearance of a satisfied mind, but at what price?

As for me, I had large goals in life and fantastic options to explore. I needed a certain personal agitation of mind so I could sift through it all and find my true self. For now, the theme of my life was Crosby against Crosby; later I'd tackle Crosby against humanity, followed by Crosby against the world.

There was one small monkey wrench in the works. My first efforts at writing had not been successful. I had trouble stringing words together. I was sure I'd write eventually, but for now, I was coming up dry. The inability to write didn't plague me too much, because in the meantime, I wasn't wasting one second. I was learning how to write by reading great books and then analyzing them down to the last letter. I didn't just read books, I scoured and investigated them; I turned them upside down and inside out. I wanted to discover the secrets of great writing. And when that time came, words would gush out of me like water out of a firehose.

I wasn't surprised when, a few minutes later, I heard the doorbell ring. I knew Brother Maston was expected, and now my thoughts about Dad Upland and writing came to a halt. It was probably my overactive imagination that made me think that two harmless references at the dinner table had deep significance, and that somehow I knew Dad or he knew me. All that would have to wait.

I had been holding Beatnik, and now I gently put him down on the bed. He was in a deep stupor of luxurious cat sleep, besotted with peace and comfort.

By the time I opened the glass-paneled door into the living room, Brother Maston was standing at the front door giving Mom and then Grandma a bear hug. He was a cross between a beatnik and a hood with all that pomaded black hair. He was wearing Levis, turned up at the cuff, and black motorcycle boots. His white T-shirt was tight around his lean carpenter's frame. He was the coolest Sunday school teacher on earth. He shook hands formally with Dad Upland and then saw me.

"Crosby, tell your Mom what the Sunday school lesson was about this morning," he said, smiling.

I was ready for the task. Brother Maston always asked that question when he saw one of his students with their parents. He never meant any harm by it, he just liked to review.

I answered promptly, "Elijah and the 850 false prophets on Mount Carmel and how one man of God stood up to them and challenged the people to stop wavering and decide who they were going to worship—God or Baal. But Ahab and Jezebel had been killing God's prophets and feeding hundreds of false prophets at their table. It was a battle for the soul of the nation: true worship or the degradation of idolatry.

"So Elijah arranged a contest. He said that the God who answered by fire is the true God. He had the false prophets go first. They laid out the sacrifice on their altar and began to shout and dance and pray and slash themselves with swords and spears till the blood flowed. But Baal paid no attention.

"Then Elijah repaired the altar of the Lord and soaked the sacrifice with water. And when he prayed, the fire from Heaven fell and burned up the sacrifice, the wood, the stones, the soil, and all the water. When the people saw all that, they fell down and cried, 'The Lord—He is God!' And then Elijah took the false prophets to the Kishon Valley and wiped them all out."

Brother Maston laughed. "You tell the story better than I do. Maybe you should teach the class next Sunday."

Brother Maston always said nice things like that to his students. And of course in class this morning, we had gotten a little off the subject and considered just how you killed off 850 false prophets in one day. The logistical problems involved in inflicting certain death on that much human flesh seemed insuperable. We finally concluded that some sort of assembly line must have been utilized, with a night crew standing by if needed.

We also pondered the ridicule Elijah had heaped on the false prophets when their god, Baal, didn't answer. Sammy Yataw asked if Elijah cussed them out like Sammy's father did to him. He pointed out that his father only swore at him after he drank twenty beers on paydays at Velma's Bar and Grille. Sammy said that at any other time his father's speech was as noble and pure and uplifting as a deacon's.

Next to Sammy was Clovis Lawson, perched by the lone window in our classroom. He was afflicted with some form of chronic indigestion which caused him to belch regularly. Either that or he subsisted on a diet of onions and spoiled meat and earthworms, because his breath was swampy and hinted of rotting carcasses and decaying vegetation. Brother Maston always insisted that Clovis sit next to the window for ventilation purposes. Clovis knew he was supposed to burp out the window. A time or two, the wind had shifted at the precise moment of a burp, causing a backdraft of his reeking breath in the loft, but the Junior boys sustained no injuries as a result. We felt that in all likelihood, Clovis had somehow built up a mysterious immunity in his system so that he remained well in spite of whatever it was that his stomach was struggling to digest. Clovis himself was as healthy as a hog; he just burped a lot.

However, his belching was a trivial matter when compared to his noxious theological reasoning concerning the Elijah story, for after Sammy Yataw's comment about the possibility of Elijah cussing out the false prophets, Clovis asked Brother Maston if we could pray the same prayer that the false prophets prayed and wait and see if Baal would answer us.

The pastor's son, Milton Barker, almost fell off his chair when Clovis suggested praying to Baal. Milton said he was going to tell his father about Clovis, but Brother Maston talked Milton out of it rather easily by reminding him that last Sunday Milton himself had angrily declared that he was going to quit coming to church altogether because the offerings were down, the same complaint we heard from his father almost every week. Of course when Pastor Barker mentioned low offerings to the congregation, he meant that as a result the church couldn't provide sufficient support for world missionaries or for our Sunday school program or for the monthly payments on his new Oldsmobile.

But Milton had a different point of view about offerings, for last Sunday he'd said, not only that he was going to quit coming to church, but he'd also added quite bitterly that low offerings meant that his father couldn't buy him a new Schwinn bicycle. "If the people in this church weren't so cheap and selfish and stingy, I'd have one by now," he said through tight lips. That was when Brother Maston had a short powwow with Milton, and you could see the light, however dimly, coming on in Milton's pimply face.

So in the end, Milton not only reconsidered snitching on Clovis but also diplomatically compromised, saying he would not mention a single word to his father about Clovis if the rest of the class would all forget his unfortunate reference to offerings, to which we all readily agreed, not because of Milton, but because we didn't want Clovis to get in trouble. He already had enough trouble with his stomach.

When Brother Maston asked me to tell Mom what my Sunday school lesson was about, I thought my answer was sufficient and accurate. But Dad Upland, to my astonishment, had tears in his eyes. He was staring at me with something like wonder in his face.

"You've got a real head on your shoulders," he said. But then he added cryptically, "I just know God gave you a gradual miracle."

Brother Maston looked at Mom and didn't say anything for a moment. But at last he blurted, "Sister Hoggard, the prophecy is well known, and you asked us all to be quiet about it, but you ought to tell Crosby—" he began, but Mom cut him off.

Her voice rose a little, and she said to Bother Maston and Dad, "Now then, since you two are guests in my home, I'm sure neither one of you wants to be impolite." There was something of a rebuke in Mom's manner. A sheepish expression suddenly spread across Brother Maston's face, and Dad gave Mom a kind, inquiring look.

She turned to me. "Crosby, why don't you and Grandma see if you can find some iced tea for our guests, please."

I know when I'm not wanted. I didn't want to hear what Mom was about to say, because it was obvious from the way she was looking at him, that Brother Maston was about to be placed at the receiving end of some very pointed words.

From the kitchen, I could hear Mom's voice, firm and controlled, telling Brother Maston something. The words were unclear, but the tone was unmistakable. I'd been on the end of Mom's sense of justice many times. She had a way of getting her point across that left you defenseless. Now Brother Maston was getting her point, and I suddenly didn't care about iced tea or good manners. I went out the kitchen back door and made my way out to the front yard. I could still hear Mom in the front room. She seemed to be winding down somewhat. Her tone was placating and reasoning and apologetic all at the same time.

I had a mood that took me from time to time. Whenever situations erupted and confusion reigned and people grew intolerable, I had to escape. No one was to blame. Dad, Mom, Grandma, and Brother Maston had nothing to do with it. Some of life's situations required firm personal steadfastness and a quick getaway. Escape had its advantages. Mom seemed to understand my mood and generally let me roam. If I didn't get away, I was going to explode. I remembered my resolution about tears and how I knew that by the strength of my own implacable willpower, I'd never be taken by convulsive tears again. So I quickly wiped the moisture from the corners of my eyes and tried not to think about my legs and feet or my father.

The sun was hot and uncomfortable, but the air smelled good. The sky was cloudless. I could see the green foothills that swept down almost to our backyard. I suddenly wished I could take a sleeping bag and live in those soft hills.

I began to walk down Orange Avenue toward Maria's house; not that I'd ever actually knock on her door. I just set out in that direction.

I knew that people felt sorry for me: poor little Crosby and his damaged legs and feet. I realized that I had just witnessed a small display of it in my front room, but I didn't want to be there as an object of pitying attention.

People didn't know it, but I considered it a betrayal when I saw the pity in their eyes. I was learning from my books all about what others around the world had suffered just in the last few decades. I was consumed with the tragedy of it all, but I wanted to do more than just feel sorry. I wanted to do something heroic to help people. I had it firsthand that millions of Jews had been systematically put to death because of their religion. I knew that two atomic bombs had ended World War II by killing two cities full of Japanese people.

Teacher said once that the total number of soldier and civilian deaths caused by the war would probably never really be known, but she guessed it was in the tens of millions. And some people thought I was to be pitied? What about all that slaughter of humanity? And what about the survivors who lost everything: family, home, possessions—even their country?

I was almost crushed by the terrible facts. But there was an image in my mind that offered me a glimmer of hope. The image was simple: a slide projector, for every month different missionaries spoke at our church, and they always set up a screen and showed color slides of the land and the people to which they had been sent. I had seen places that were blasted with sweltering heat or periodically submerged under torrential rains or almost frozen under a sheet of ice the year round. The people on the screen had suffered through wars and famines and droughts and disease and periods of near starvation.

And yet, every missionary wanted to be back where those people were. Dangerous conditions didn't stop them—the people were the thing. The missionaries always said God had sent them to the people up on the screen and that they loved them. They'd actually weep when they said that they couldn't wait to return to the mission field. To me, the missionary proved there was a thing called the peopleness of people. That's what we all are. We all have peopleness in common. And people need help, not suspicion or war or bigotry. And since I'm a people, I figured that there must be something I could do to remedy suffering and anguish and distress. Doing something about injustice and trouble was one of my many goals.

Dov Landau had the right idea: improvise and survive and fight back and resist the evil in the world. I wanted to be partners with Dov and help Jews get into Israel. I wished I could have been there for the Joads, helping them to get jobs in California, and I know I could have found a way to lift Francie and Neeley out of poverty and to save their father's life.

Walking up Orange Avenue now toward Alcazar Street, I thought about my gift of grim determination and how I could not be stopped. A man with a noble purpose is indefatigable and unwavering. I knew what I wanted. I wasn't Crosby Hoggard, the singing pig, an object of pity; I was Crosby Hoggard, the famous writer, the saver of lives. I planned on maybe two or three years in the Aliyah Bet, smuggling Jews with cleverly forged documents into Israel where there was no possibility of confiscated businesses, no yellow star of David armbands to wear, and no ovens waiting. Then I'd visit prisons and tell the inmates that Moses and David and Paul were all murderers, but God picked them up, changed them, and took their mess and gave them a message. Then God did unimaginably great things with their lives. Next I'd travel to every continent and prove the peopleness of people to every villager, citizen, and inhabitant, and I'd tell them that since God made us all people, we needed to help each other. I'd be Crosby, the giver of opportunities, the solver of insuperable problems, the imparter of hope and help from Heaven. People would give up their small ambitions when they heard me. They would conceive larger aspirations in life. I'd be like a father to them, the kind of father that knows how to love and protect and provide for his children and gives them strong hugs every day.

Finally, I'd write the story of my life, using composite characters based on real people I'd known, and the world would be so glad I wrote it all down, and they would give me their grateful approval and acceptance.

The sunlight in my face felt like I had stuck my head in an oven. Sometimes my thinking about things made me feel tired and worn-out, like a long distance runner after a 50-mile run.

I was at Alcazar Street now, and I hesitated there for a moment. Then I judged that because of the heat and what with me feeling tired, I might as well turn right and head in the general direction of Maria's house. I was thinking that perhaps I might sit down for a short rest if she were home.

She was not only home, but there she was, standing at the gate. Her front yard, as small as it was, had more cactus per square inch than any other yard in town. The colors ranged from light greens to deep browns and gray. The cactus plants were all sizes and shapes and varieties. There were low-growing round cactus plants and tall needle-studded dark-green cactus. It was not a haphazard arrangement. Maria's father did yard work for a living, and I saw him quite frequently in his modified Chevy sedan heading up and down Orange Avenue. The Chevy was a 1949 model. Its entire back seat and trunk area were cut away, replaced by homemade wooden sides and a pickup truck bed. Several shovels, rakes, and hoes were affixed to the sides, standing at attention like garden soldiers. He must have been a gardener of prodigious skills because the cactus in his front yard had no equal in Monte Vista.

Maria was standing there watching me approach her house. She had a beaming smile on her face. Her hair shined, and her brown eyes and dark complexion seemed a perfect combination. She was wearing what I supposed was her Sunday best: a light-blue dress and black shoes, a matching blue ribbon in her hair.

"Crosby, you look tired," she said pleasantly. She wasn't being unkind; I was tired. She opened the little gate. "Come and sit in the shade."

There was a wooden bench under the one shade tree in the yard. I sat down, laying my crutch against the bench. Maria went in the door of her home and emerged a minute later with iced tea the way I like it—in a Mason jar with lots of ice.

I took one long drink and then set the Mason jar down next to me on the bench. I looked at Maria and asked, "Do you think old people should get married?"

She gave me a shy look. "As long as they are in love," she said softly.

Now I knew for sure that Grandma and Dad were headed for trouble. How could they be in love after a walk around the block? This was worse than an arranged marriage, where the bride and groom had no say about who marries whom. What if you didn't love your dearly intended, but it had been arranged that you had to walk the aisle with her?

Then the heat got to my brain and without quite grasping where I was or to whom I was speaking, I mused out loud, "I wonder what it feels like to be in love?"

Maria blushed a little. "I think it's more than a feeling," she said in a helpful tone. "It's deeper somewhere in the heart of a man and a woman. Don't you think so?"

I nearly jumped up and ran. Had I just said what I thought I said? To Maria? I knew I had to respond. So recovering quickly, I said cleverly, "I've read about it in books." I was nodding my head vigorously. "Characters are always falling in love, like it's some kind of pit you can never crawl out of, or like quicksand and you just get swallowed up in its depths and then you suffocate."

At home I never even said "I love you" to Mom or Grandma. They knew I loved them, and so obviously I didn't need to say it all the time. And it was true that I sang, "Oh, how I love Jesus," as was the custom on Sunday morning, but it was a song for boys and girls to march to—I never thought about the words. I just marched off to my Sunday school class while we were singing. I once wondered why Jesus wanted me to tell him anything since he already knew everything, being part of the Trinity, and therefore having access to all knowledge. So it was a little like Mom and Grandma: why should I say "I love you" when he already knew the answer?

But Maria wasn't talking about family love or religious love. She meant romantic love between a man and a woman or maybe even between a boy and a girl who were sitting together on a bench in the girl's front yard. This conversation was getting out of hand. I had to do something about it.

I patted Maria on the hand. "Thank you for the tea," I said brightly. I stood up as if to go. Another escape.

But Maria wasn't through with the cross-examination. "In my opinion, real-life love is different from what you read about in books. Don't you agree?"

I sat back down. "Wait a minute," I said defensively. "That all depends on what books you're reading. Some writers can describe love very realistically. Like Scarlett and Rhett." And then I paused abruptly. "Although now that I recall the situation," I continued thoughtfully, "I don't think Scarlett ever caught on to how much Rhett really did love her. She was a very stubborn Southern Belle, and if she had just loved Rhett the way she should have, everything would have turned out all right, and love would have won the day. So my case is proved: real love is portrayed in books, but sometimes you have to write an extra chapter in your imagination."

I got up once again. This time I was leaving for sure. I tucked my crutch under my arm.

But Maria had one last question. "Crosby," she said frankly, "why did you come to my house today?"

She wasn't supposed to ask questions. It's unsettling to be confronted with the unanswerable. The unspoken rule between us was that I did the talking and Maria listened closely and then gave me her approval.

So I answered smoothly, "I was out for a walk and you happened to be out front and so I slowed down and you said I looked tired and that I should come in and sit down in the shade. And so I did."

I thought I carried it off rather well. There were no declarations and no complications conveyed in my response.

Maria blinked her brown eyes. Sometimes she was shy, but other times she could be downright forward.

She now said pointedly, "I like to talk to you, Crosby, because you always have interesting things to say. You can talk to me anytime." And then she added quite boldly, "Crosby, could you sit down again and listen to me for a minute?"

My eyes widened a little, and I nodded my head slowly. "Sure," I said, taking my place once again on the bench. I still had escaping on my mind, but it wasn't so bad a thing being told what to do by Maria. Besides, I was curious about the direction our conversation had taken, and I was wondering how I could get myself out of this predicament. It was almost like I was being confronted.

Part of my mind recognized that I was on her turf and had therefore given her certain rights. She hadn't sounded angry when she asked me to sit down. If anything, I noted a certain feisty fondness in her tone.

And so now I looked at her. She had the smoothest complexion I had ever seen in a girl. Her eyes were clear and brown and radiant. But there was also a trace of sadness in her expression that I wondered about. I had never given her such a lingering appraisal, and I admitted she passed inspection.

Then it occurred to me that while I was surveying Maria, she was assessing me, though I couldn't begin to guess her standard for comparison nor where I might fall on the scale she was using. I didn't think I was particularly handsome. I wasn't tall or athletic or engaging in my features. My mirror image always showed me too much blond hair and blue eyes. I weighed about sixty-five pounds, and I had blond eyebrows that I thought made me look like a ghost. Aside from the wrong body shape, coloring, height, and weight, I wasn't too gruesome to behold.

I was sitting on the bench like Maria had asked me to do, and she was taking her own sweet time in getting to the point. But at last she said, "I think you have a nice personality, Crosby."

She was off to a good start. I had made it a habit to work on self-improvement and the personal cultivation of all the finest human characteristics described in my books. Lately, I had been applying myself to the determination of the Maccabees, the resourcefulness of Dov Landau, the adventurous spirit of Huck and Tom, and the cleverness of Bomba the jungle boy. In short, I had freely availed myself of these and other attributes, all of which had been so clearly portrayed in the lives of the bravest fictional characters ever set down on the printed page.

But nothing had prepared me for Maria's next statement. She smiled and said, "You're too hard on yourself, and you need friends like everybody else. I shouldn't be the only friend you have. You're clever and good and funny. And if I enjoy being with you, other people will too."

I couldn't have been more surprised if she had sprouted wings and flapped her way to the moon.

But since I'm never at a loss for appropriate words, I said briskly, "I think I understand what you're driving at and I think some people would call what you've just described as an inferiority complex and I've read about complexes, but I have reasons behind my actions which are not always readily apparent, which brings me to the whole idea of friends, and I'd say that I need to observe human behavior more than I need to enjoy it in the form of friendship."

I paused and took a breath. I couldn't blurt out that I wanted to write stories and that I believed in the peopleness of people and that those were the only two things I wanted to do something about.

An adept rejoinder throws people off-balance, which I was shamelessly attempting to do with Maria. So I had thrown some verbal dust in her face.

But it didn't work, for Maria now switched tactics: she abruptly asked me a question about a subject that she knew was a forbidden topic between us. She asked me gently, "Do you remember when my father and your father used to go to Velma's?"

I leaped to my feet. I'd never liked the mention of Velma's Bar and Grille. It was a common lowdown evil beer joint, located up a winding road in the foothills of Monte Vista. I hated the place. It was where ruined people went to drink. People of value don't go to beer joints, as everyone knows.

I shoved my crutch under my arm, and I had taken a step toward the gate when I remembered I hadn't answered Maria. I turned around and looked at her, still sitting on the bench. She looked a little startled; at what, I didn't know. Probably she realized that she shouldn't have brought up Velma's because it was such a despicable place and a blot on our town, and she was ashamed of her father for going there.

"I'll see you tomorrow," I said easily. "I have to go home and get ready for church." I didn't want Maria to feel bad about bringing up Velma's Bar and Grille, so I added, "You look real nice today." But she didn't say anything, and that surprised look was still on her face.

Maria didn't get up when I left her front yard as far as I knew, because I didn't turn around to check and see. I just hurriedly went out her gate and set my face for home.

The sun had taken a slant to the west by now, and I wasn't feeling as much heat as I did when I began my walk through the neighborhood. And as I headed for home, I told myself that Maria meant well. She never teased me or acted like she was better than me. But today, she had gone over a line of protocol which should never have been crossed. It was probably a case of simple misjudgment on her part. I didn't blame her. She had actually brought up Velma's Bar and Grille.

Velma's was a sign of decadence and a symbol of all that was wrong with people. Men and women gathered there like it was the devil's church, and attendance was mandatory. The people got drunk and cussed and told dirty jokes there. The men flirted openly with vile women. I know this to be the truth because Pastor Barker, along with the popular theme of the inherent vileness of women, also preached against the abominations of bars and beer joints, cussing, wicked movies, beauty parlors, a Catholic in the White House, and rock and roll music. So there you had it. And the culmination of all sin was a depraved beer joint, because within those walls you had vile women, foul language, a jukebox playing wicked music, the menace of alcohol, and probably many Catholic voters. I could think of no greater single evil, and Pastor Barker made these truths plainer every time he preached.

When I went out Maria's front gate, I had turned left, which meant I was now taking a different route home. Alcazar Street led me to Byrne Avenue where I turned right. The sunlight was now on my back and not so hot as before. After a few blocks, I could turn right up Granada Street, and then after a short distance, I'd arrive home, and I could slip into the house through my own back porch entrance.

Too many things had happened today, and I didn't know if church attendance was within reason. A man has only so much strength, and mine was stretched out to the limit. I felt worn-out.

But my tired mind still had some things to go over. I thought about Dad Upland's short sermon and collapse in the pulpit this morning, his reviving and subsequent march around the block, followed by a marriage proposal to my grandmother. That should have been enough turmoil for one day, but then I had dinner with Dad and a quick visit with Brother Maston which drove me to escape from the house.

It suddenly occurred to me that I had made two escapes today, one from home and the other from Maria's front yard. I wasn't being a good writer-in-training, running from situations that made me uncomfortable. I reasoned that people should be more sensitive to me in the future and not furnish the cause that forced me to high-tail it out of there. Someday I was going to write a blistering story about this very thing, and the theme would be man's inhumanity to man, featuring me as the man on whom all the inhumanity was perpetrated.

Then Maria's words came back to me. She had said that I had a nice personality. It made me feel good that Maria recognized things about me that other people refused to acknowledge. Her reference to Velma's was unfortunate, but understandable. Probably Maria knew what a malevolent place Velma's was and wished her father would stay away from there and give up his evil drinking. Men drank at Velma's and then stumbled home to do stupid things. The clear proof of that was the way Francie and Neeley's father drank and then died young, leaving his children without a father's love.

It punctured my balloon a little that I found many of my book people fascinating even though they were hard drinkers. But good writing, I told myself, sometimes glosses over the real consequences of some behaviors. So in all likelihood, the hard drinking of my book people had been exaggerated for maximum dramatic effect, a use of literary license that I regarded as justifiable.

The fact remained, though, that Velma's Bar and Grille actually existed and that Velma herself was undoubtedly a trendsetter even among the very worst collection of vile women. I blamed her for keeping her beer joint open and held her personally responsible for luring potential victims inside her abominable establishment.

When I finally reached home, I quietly slipped in the house through my own entrance and waited, listening for any sounds. It didn't seem like anyone was home, which most likely meant Mom and Grandma were napping, but they'd be up soon. It was getting close to the time for us to leave for church, and I only had a few minutes to prepare myself.

I looked around for Beatnik, but he was nowhere to be found. He was probably out stalking birds or squirrels or rabbits. He was a fierce hunter.

The cabinet with the ruined hinges held most of my books. Mom had a few *Reader's Digest Condensed Books* around the living room which I occasionally glanced at. But here on the back porch were my very good friends. Every now and then, I sheepishly admitted to myself that books were my best, most loyal friends. I had been on an unwavering, dogged reading jag for two or three years, and there were no signs of a slowdown on the horizon. In fact, I felt like I was just getting started on great reading. And now to be prepared for tonight's sermon, I was going to need something powerful to occupy my mind. So I grabbed my favorite blue-covered paperback out of the cabinet, and then quiet as a whisper, I eased the doors shut.

I occasionally noticed colors around me, like a blue sky or dark-green foothills or a golden sunset, but the covers of my paperbacks were different. Those colors stood out. They were firmly imprinted on my mind, and I associated the color blue with great reading.

I now opened the book and began to revel in the printed word. How I sympathized with Karen Clement's struggle and suffering during World War II, leaving her family in Cologne, Germany, and being sent to Denmark to live with Ange and Meta Hansen. And why had her parents sent her away? It was the unrelenting hatred of the Nazis against the Jews that forced her parents to make the painful and difficult decision to send their daughter to a safe place. And then later, after surviving the ravages of war, she had met Dov Landau at a refugee camp in Crete, and he was smitten with her loveliness.

After a few more minutes of reading, I put the book back in the cabinet and then went and washed my face. My mind was now ready, and my instincts freshly honed for a Sunday night church service.

I wondered briefly about who would speak tonight. Was Dad Upland still around, and if so, was he going to make another attempt at preaching? But regardless of who was going to preach, I planned to sit in one of the back pews during the service so no one would notice me, and, if it became necessary, I'd be prepared to bolt from the building.

Sunday night church was different from Sunday morning. Mainly it was louder. Everything from the testifying to the preaching, from the praying to the singing of the choir—everything raised the decibel level exponentially. I held the belief that it was the night air or something in the water or the fear of facing another Monday that completely demolished whatever decorum we had. It seemed like there was a note of desperation in the service, people trying to extract some measure of hope from the resources at hand. So they whooped it up, like a sailor having one last fling before being shipped off to war.

A case in point was our choir director, the pastor's brother, Gale Barker. He was tall and skinny and thin-lipped and too fussy to be around for more than a minute at a time. His face showed fastidious care—a thin, neatly trimmed mustache, wispy eyebrows, and dark, mournful eyes. He was mostly sorrowful in or out church, and when he tried to smile, it was like watching a Pharisee caught in a furious debate with himself as to whether he should or should not cast the first stone at an adulterous woman. His smile was just that unnatural and strained.

He had a silent, withdrawn wife and two pale little sons who hardly spoke. He typified the kind of desperation I'd noticed in church. It didn't seem like he or his wife or his sons were particularly happy, but the entire family came to church every time the doors were opened.

He led the choir with a certain peculiarity. If there was no soprano to hit the high notes, he'd sing it. Music, therefore, took a real shellacking on Sunday nights. Everyone knew it was his voice hitting those screechy soprano notes, and it never sounded like anything other than a skinny and mournful male choir director trying, but never quite succeeding, to achieve a certain high note. Tarzan carried a better tune.

But that was nothing compared to Brother Gale's Sunday night run. When the service reached the right pitch—loud, overwrought, incoherent—Brother Gale would take off like a shot, hollering down one aisle and up another. Pastor Barker's hairdo didn't frighten young children half as much as his brother's run. We all suffered an agonized sense of expectancy every Sunday night, waiting for and dreading the moment when Brother Gale would explode into action, bellowing down the aisles. Several times I'd prayed fervently that Brother Gale would transfer his church membership to Velma's where he belonged.

But Brother Gale was only one man. There was another set of eccentricities that characterized several church members, namely the shakes, the jerks, and the kicks.

Pastor Barker and Brother Santiago usually got the jerks Sunday nights. I had learned by close observation that the jerks were a sort of sudden, spasmodic heaving of the whole body, which was over in a second or two. If the jerks became more frequent—coming in waves—then you called that the shakes, although there was a thin line between the two manifestations, and you had to be rather fluid in your definitions.

Pastor Barker was something of a pioneer in all of this for he could demonstrate an amazing control while jerking. He'd announce that the hand of the Lord was upon him and then go into an extended twitching while preaching. It then sounded like he was speaking underwater, his speech was so garbled, yet he maintained a real composure at the same time. Others, following his example, would attempt the same dual manifestation of shaking and testifying, but they were genuinely unintelligible. They simply could not pull it off with Pastor's aplomb.

Our church was, in fact, somewhat divided on the issue of jerks and kicks and shakes. Generally, those who preferred kicking sat on the right side of the church and those prone to jerking sat on the left. Overall, kicking involved simply what its name implied: a small kick from the knee hinge down, though the kick itself was not directed at anyone in particular. You just got so blessed that your foot leaped forward almost on its own. But those who jerked would twitch with one sudden jolt, and then it was all over. Proper etiquette dictated that prolonged jerks were termed the shakes, an important distinction, for quite frequently Sister Fitts had the jerks Sunday mornings and the shakes Sunday nights. Everyone agreed it was an unusual development. I was personally at a loss as to the established conventions. She was exhibiting bad form here, for she was far better at the shakes than the jerks, and she should have stayed with her strong points because she was a big woman who could easily shake for two. Her husband, Charles, never closed his eyes when his wife was shaking. One good sustained quiver from her prodigious body had on occasion bumped him and sent him backpedaling into the pew. He always got right back up, evidence that no damage had been done, though I noticed that he routinely edged a few inches away from his wife after that.

My role in church on Sunday nights was the same as it was at school: I was spectator, rugged individualist, logician, and touch-stone. All the others were Don Quixotes, and I was Sancho Panza. Sometimes I was a bewildered Sancho, for occasionally things hap-pened which caught me off guard. For instance, one Sunday night, Sister Nellie Dupont, a thin, rather meek older woman, began to emit canine sounds. With her head tilted back, she barked and growled until she finally resolved it all into a smooth baying like a basset hound. But she calmed down a few seconds later when Brother Maston left his pew and began to pat her on the head. I wanted to tell her to sit up so I could toss her a dog biscuit, but who would think it is necessary to bring a milk-bone to church?

Another time my Sunday school partner, Sammy Yataw, con-fessed in a broken voice that he loved how Little Richard could wail. He said he'd been practicing the art of wailing at home, but his mother made him stop because it was scaring the neighborhood cats.

Sammy had set a truly ominous precedent, implying by his con-fession that perhaps there were other boys present with something to confess, like the reading of forbidden literature. So I sat very still while several of the brethren tended to Sammy.

At first, the brethren were thrown off by the reference to wail-ing. I heard one of them say that it was probably some new manifes-tation, and that it should be considered as an alternative to jerking and shaking. They were all looking at each other, standing there in a circle up front around Sammy. It appeared to me that they were wondering who should make the first attempt at wailing.

But then Sammy offered a short explanation as to the nature and type and quality of wailing Little Richard engaged in, and the brethren immediately began to pray feverishly for the boy, and as a result, Sammy swore off all Little Richard recordings. Later, Sammy told me he felt much better and that from now on, he was going to stick with Elvis, who himself was a thorny doctrinal problem.

The fact was that Sammy hadn't resolved anything by switching over to Elvis, for almost every Sunday night we heard confessions from teenage backsliders who during the past week had yielded to temptation and listened to Elvis on the radio. The problem was we had heard that Elvis as a young man had sung in the choir at his church in Tupelo, Mississippi. This meant that he might be one of us, even right down to the same denomination. For we could all see with our own eyes that his antics on stage were simply mild imitations of the shaking and jerking he had learned at Sunday night church services in Tupelo. Taken as a whole, it was a sticky issue. The teenage girls in our church loved Elvis and frequently prayed for him, along with Tony Curtis, the entire cast of *77 Sunset Strip* and Bobby Darin, but Elvis had the upper hand since he was an eligible bachelor with a church background.

I got an earful on the girls' thinking about all this one night after church. A bunch of them had gathered together out front, and I couldn't help but overhear their excited talk. It went like this: Elvis might come to town because he might know someone here and then he might feel a deep need to worship and might come to our church and might notice one of the girls and might fall in love with her and might marry her.

I stood there dumfounded listening to the girls hanging their lives on the word *might*, which is related to the word *maybe*, and when you put the two words together, the best you can get is a giant "maybe-might." So their destinies were all about impossibilities and not inevitabilities.

The whole thing disgusted me. The likelihood that Elvis Presley would show up at our church some Sunday night was about the same as it would be for Nikita Khrushchev to arrive some Sunday morning and teach my Sunday school class.

And undoubtedly a large number of the girls were secretly praying for Elvis to show up, for I noticed that several of them dressed up especially nice for Sunday night services just in case Elvis walked in. There was a contingent that held out for a visit from Ricky Nelson, since it was widely known that he actually lived in California with his mother and father and older brother, and he only had to drive a relatively short distance to visit us, as opposed to Elvis, who would have to travel across several state borders to get here.

This night, however, we had no visits from Elvis or Ricky. I sat in my back pew, wondering who our speaker would be since no one was sitting up on the platform with Pastor Barker except his skinny brother who was trying to catch his breath, for he had just bolted up and down the aisles like a Jackrabbit on fire. My ears were still ringing from the high-pitched bellowing that accompanied his run. And now you could hear Brother Gale making noises that sounded like a pressure release valve being adjusted on a steam engine.

Pastor Barker took it all in stride. He now came to the pulpit and announced some sad news. He looked almost as mournful as his brother. He said heavily, "It seems that we have a shortage in our giving this week due to the abruptness of the ending of our service this morning. Many of you left this morning and took your offering envelopes with you. Now I want you to ask yourself, how much should I give? It is a shameful thing to withhold your money from God because He, after all, gives to you, don't you see? I want all you people to look deeply into your hearts and wallets and purses and don't forget your pockets and your money belts and ask yourself another question: 'How much do I care about my church and the upcoming election and the possibility of a Catholic under the direct orders of the Pope in Rome telling me what to do because I failed to give? We have expenses which must be met in order to keep our doors open. Some of you could give an extra ten or twenty dollars, and some of you could give a hundred dollars on tonight. Some of you people already have next week's pay check spent and haven't even asked yourself the simple question, 'How much does God get?' I want you to dig deep—really, really dig now and give sacrificially for the glory of God so that we don't have to close the doors of our beloved church and that for which it stands."

Pastor went on and on. When it came to answered prayer, Pastor Barker believed that God would answer immediately with an exact dollar amount if you asked him, "How much should I give?" Other prayers took a little longer for the Almighty to respond to, such as "Where should I live? Who should I marry? What should I do with my life? What is my destiny? Why am I depressed all the time? Why did my father die? When will I know life is worth living? Why is there so much suffering in the universe?"

With those questions, you were exhorted to have patience and wait on the Lord for an answer, but when it came to how much money to give, you evidently heard a voice from heaven, which always announced the exact figure down to the last cent.

Pastor finally wrapped up his passionate appeal for the night's offering, and then the church deacons came forward and stood shoulder to shoulder up front facing the congregation. Each one of them was holding a shiny silver-colored offering tray lined in green felt. Pastor offered a short but pointed prayer, and the deacons passed among us.

I was enthralled with the proceedings. I always asked God about giving, and since I never heard a voice telling me the amount, I logically assumed I was receiving a negative answer, so I never gave a cent. I did this as an experiment. Was the Church going to close because I didn't give? Was my giving going to provide Milton Barker with a new Schwinn? That possibility made my blood boil. Personally I didn't believe Milton could peddle a bike and think at the same time.

I knew my Mom and Grandma took Pastor's words at face value and faithfully gave in the regular church offering each Sunday. Every now and then, there were other opportunities to give, which usually revolved around Pastor Barker. At times he needed extra money for car repairs or money to pay for his attendance at important church conferences, which sometimes convened as far away as Stockton, or even Fresno. When those occasions arose, one of the church elders came to the pulpit and made the appeal on Pastor's behalf. And while the elder was presenting the case for more money, Pastor Barker would sit quietly in his chair behind the pulpit with a humble, vulnerable, hopelessly lost look on his face. The money always came in.

On the other hand, when Mom had a special need, Pastor was quick to pray for her faith not to fail, and he always encouraged her to trust God for finances. No elder made an appeal on her behalf. And it apparently never occurred to Pastor Barker that what's good for the goose is even better for the gander.

My experience in not giving a cent yielded valuable data. For one thing, the church never closed, and for another, Milton never got his new Schwinn, which was a very gratifying outcome to me.

While offering plates were passing up and down the aisles, Sister Barker played "I Shall Not Be Moved," a lively tune that put me in mind of eviction notices. I had a good ear for hymnology. I divided church music up into two main categories: the lively sentimental, and the sloppy sentimental. During the week I secretly listened to the radio, from which I heard Fats Domino, Elvis Presley, and Little Richard. There was a comparison to be made between church music and radio music. On weekdays I could almost smell the blueberries up that hill, and I could almost see the dingy, forlorn façade of that hotel where everyone was suffering from heartbreak, and Miss Molly must have been even nicer than Sister Barker. So why would I want to wander into a garden where the dew was still on the roses? And I wasn't quite sure what a sheave was and far less did I want to bring one in.

I'm nothing if not analytical, and I recognized cow-eyed sentimentality when it came lowing musically at my door. Granted, "A Mighty Fortress is Our God" coined a real image in my imagination. I could see myself stationed in the fortress as God's mortar man, lobbing shell after shell on the devil's headquarters.

Once the offering was taken, Brother Barker bounced into the pulpit. At long last I'd find out who would speak tonight. I looked across the center aisle to where Mom and Grandma were sitting together. Dad Upland wasn't sitting with them, nor was he up on the platform with Pastor Barker.

Then it suddenly hit me: why was I so concerned about who was going to speak tonight? It occurred to me that I had the same sense of desperation as everyone else. I wanted to extract some hope, some explanation as to why things in my life were the way they were, because maybe the people here and their shenanigans held the secret to that knowledge.

I more or less dreaded school. I loved my home. And church had my attention because the people were eccentric and familiar and provocative and entertaining. They also kept a close vigil over each other. My reading didn't exactly protect me, but here in my pew, I knew that I was surrounded by a sense of practical guardianship, sometimes cloyingly executed and sometimes not, from the people I observed every Sunday.

The realization brought me up short. What about my role as spectator? I wanted to be a rugged individualist. I had observed over time that Mom and Grandma were quietly tended to by some of the people we knew at church who routinely just happened to show up at the right moments. Brother Maston always did tune-ups and oil changes on our car and then waved his hand in dismissal when Mom tried to pay him. And Grandma made several dollars from time to time by selling homemade pies to church members. That was how it worked for Mom and Grandma.

But everything has its pros and cons. The pros here were for Mom and Grandma, and most of the cons fell on me. I truly liked being a spectator. I didn't want anyone's help. Being a rugged individualist and a writer-in-training, I needed to cultivate a moody, bittersweet, cynical, world-weary existence. I wanted a writer's life. I wanted to smoke Lucky Strikes and ruffle feathers with my profound, insightful writing. It was all about self-sufficiency. I wanted to sit hunched over a typewriter, clad in a flannel shirt and jeans, fists clenched at my temples, luring the next impassioned word out of my fertile mind. I considered myself above the events around me; I was a spectator, taking meticulous mental notes for future use in one of my novels. Brother, was I going to wallop the world with what I knew. I'd write essays about the great theme of the peopleness of people and show everyone that Ma Joad, even when she hardly had enough food for her own family, was right when she shared her stew with the hungry children in the migrant worker's camp. And I'd prove that occasionally extraordinary measures were required; sometimes people needed to assert their peopleness: like the time when three hundred Jewish children, who had been made refugees by World War II, were being held behind a barbed wire fence in a displaced person's camp on the island of Crete. Yet one day they escaped to a ship in the harbor and then went on a hunger strike, which eventually forced the British to allow the ship to get underway to Israel and freedom.

I had been sitting a long time on a hard wooden pew. I shifted around a little to get the blood circulating again. I figured that the combination of wondering with some curiosity about tonight's speaker and considering the fact that being a spectator is arduous work—those two things—joined to make me more keyed up than usual. But now I felt a certain resignation. I realized that whoever was going to speak tonight was going to speak. If it was to be Dad Upland, then so be it. Dad didn't owe me anything, and I didn't owe him anything.

And in the end, after all my agitation, it turned out that Pastor Barker did the preaching. His topic was Bible prophecy. The working title of the sermon was, "Has God Washed His Hands of the Whole Shebang or Should We Allow Godless Communism to Dictate Our Morality Under the Abomination of a Catholic President?"

The title, though cumbersome, did not convey the many nuances Pastor could stuff into a single address. He started in the book of Revelation, which served as a springboard for his favorite themes and pet peeves. After reading one verse, whose connection to the sermon's title disappeared in a cloud of smoke, Pastor was off and running and so was my imagination. This was where my reading material usually occupied me. Chasing the meaning of a message and trying to track down Pastor's connecting links from one thought to another was work for a herd of philosophers, logicians, and state mental health workers. I always pursued the logical steps of human behavior in the stories I read where links between thoughts and actions actually existed, but Pastor's sermons baffled me.

So now I resorted to thoughts about fiction, where my favorite characters reacted to life with some degree of logic and consistency. Unlike Pastor Barker's scattered, illogical freewheeling romp in and around the fringes of his sermon topic, all my novels adhered to a strict sense of cause and effect. The characters were my favorites precisely because of their conflicted and dead end, point-of-no-return, no resolution lives, but at least they were logical about it.

I suddenly felt like steam must be spouting from my ears. I was thinking too much, ignoring the evening's sermon and having too much fun with my own thoughts. I loved my books, even the ones that everybody I knew considered to be dirty novels. There were things in them that I wasn't supposed to know about, and when I put them all together, it formed quite an impressive list of life activities, all of which were deemed to be dirty, off-limits, and unmentionable: things like murder and other violent acts, rape, degenerate sex, and anything else that was sleazy, lewd, smutty, suggestive, or depraved. And of course vile women.

The most offensive item on the list was the wrong use of sex, a category which at one time made up almost all of my knowledge about sex. Mom never brought the subject up, and Pastor Barker grew red in the face when he spoke about filth, degeneracy, abominations, and sex, usually in the same breath and always in that order.

I am nothing if not curious. I had once checked out a book on human sexuality from the library. Reading it filled in several blanks in my education, especially the chapter on love and sex, which settled the ultimate issue for me. I seldom heard Pastor Barker connect the two ideas of sex and love, though occasionally he did refer to marriage and sex in a grudging, indignant way. It was rather comical. Did he think that church membership meant dehumanization? I wondered once if I should give a copy of the book I'd read to Pastor Barker. It said that the entire human race needed more education on the facts of life. It went so far as to say that the marriage relationship was designed to be healthy and wholesome and sweet.

I definitely didn't need to give any reading material on the subject of love and marriage to Brother Maston. It wasn't so much what he said about marriage from our Sunday school quarterly, because our lesson books never got near the subject. Rather, it was what he said about marriage on a personal level, and it was up to us Junior boys to play our cards right and get Brother Maston off the week's lesson so he would bring up a topic near and dear to our hearts: how we could find someone to marry who was as nice as Sister Maston.

Brenda Maston was plump and pretty and full of humor. She apparently never wanted to be away from Brother Maston. She clung tenaciously to his arm entering and leaving church. She had a sense of possessiveness and outright ownership over her husband that made the Junior boys class hope and pray that she had plenty of younger sisters. It didn't hurt matters that she had blonde hair, dainty feet, radiant blue eyes, and a ravishing overbite like Dinah Shore.

Brother Maston wasn't tactless. In fact, he was very careful, sensitive, and diplomatic when it came to talking about Brenda. He never said anything scandalous about her in Sunday school, but he did display a dreamy, faraway look in his eyes when he recalled their honeymoon, which was the keyword we used to get him off that day's lesson and on to more practical matters. So if he was teaching on the Bride of Christ or the Marriage Supper of the Lamb—subjects that at least mentioned certain key words—all one of us had to do was ask about his honeymoon, and, beginning with his courtship of Brenda, he'd go on and describe their many dates and his proposal and their marriage ceremony and finally get to the point—their honeymoon trip all the way out of town to the City of Gilroy.

Each time he told the story, he went a little further in the details. Right now we were up to the registration desk at the Butterfly Motel. The story had stalled out at that point. Someday we were going to find a way to get him to start in on the next chapter, but just how to do that had us all stumped. Sunday school with Brother Maston was an engrossing experience and held a real note of suspense and anticipation for all the Junior boys.

Suddenly I became conscious of movement around me. Church was over. I had missed most of Pastor Barker's sermon and every word of the benediction. I was exhausted from the day's activities and wanted to go home.

I went outside into the warm night air, sat down on the steps, and clamped my hands on both sides of my head. Sunday night church took a lot out of me. As usual I was waiting for Mom and Grandma to emerge from the front doors so we could walk home together.

But then Brother Maston came out and asked me if I'd like to go with he and his wife to Foster's Freeze for ice cream. I was stunned by the invitation, for I'd never been asked to go anywhere with the older folks after church, even though it was a Sunday night ritual for many of them. And at that moment, my head was still aching and buzzing from too much thinking. It seemed simple enough. A huge ice-cream cone would be the perfect cure for what ailed me, far better than an aspirin.

I looked at it this way: I figured that everyone was stirred up after a rousing Sunday night sermon, and the way to recover some sense of normalcy was through dairy products. A good, piercing ice-cream headache would bring your feet back down to earth in a hurry.

I wanted to go with the Mastons, but first there was the small technicality of getting permission from Mom. When I asked her, she gave me a dubious look.

"I don't want you out late, Crosby," she said. "You have school tomorrow, and I don't want you to start the week all tired out."

School! It was on the tip of my tongue to say thanks for the reminder, but instead I said earnestly, "Brother Maston has the nicest car in town and I'll be safe and he has to swing a hammer tomorrow so he won't keep me out late."

Actually Brother Maston had the fastest car in town, but saying that to Mom would give the wrong impression, as though we were about to break the track record by racing out to Steven's Creek Boulevard and then flooring it all the way over to the Foster's Freeze in Sunnyvale.

Looking a little skeptical, Mom finally gave me a reluctant nod.

I was in the front seat of Brother Maston's 1955 Chevy before Mom could change her mind. It was rumored that there was an experimental Corvette engine under the hood, and that Brother Maston had spent too much money on frivolous accessories for a simple vehicle. The Chevy was white, two-door post, with tuck and roll interior. It was equipped with glass pack mufflers and Lake pipes, a combination that growled mellow and sweet through the neighborhood. Brother Maston had requested prayer in church several times for release from speed demons, and as far as anyone knew, he was now completely cured and drove as sedately and contritely as if he were the lead car in a funeral procession.

So with Sister Maston between us, Brother Maston pulled away from the curb.

He looked over at me and said happily, "Hang on, Crosby." I gripped the edge of the dashboard as Brother Maston turned right on

Steven's Creek Boulevard. He hit second gear as smooth as butter. He was also speeding up a little.

Brenda said warningly, "Jerry, remember your promise."

"I'm cured of speeding, Bren," he said hastily.

I wanted to add to the conversation, so I sat back and said amiably, "Someday I'd like to visit Gilroy's Butterfly Motel." It was good to know a little about people's lives, so that polite conversation could be conducted along familiar and interesting lines.

Brenda was suddenly very still, and Brother Maston looked studiously in the rearview mirror for several seconds. There was a prolonged pause.

Looking piercingly at Brother Maston, Brenda finally said, "I see Sunday school lessons are getting off the week's topic again." She whacked Brother Maston on the arm, but not so hard that it would hurt.

Brother Maston ducked his head a little and then threw a quick look at his wife. "Don't worry, Bren," he said reassuringly, "Crosby's just kidding." He gave me a quick warning glance. It was subtle, but I got the message.

"It's all right, Sister Maston," I said. "I don't know anything about what took place after the registration desk."

Sister Maston stared at me openmouthed for a second and then began to laugh so hard and loud that I thought the car was going to shake.

When she calmed down, she said, "Crosby, you're the greatest kid I've ever known. And I'm so glad my little brother knows you."

"You have a brother?" I asked politely.

"Well, my maiden name is Brenda Winston, and my brother tells me you're in his class."

"Clyde Winston is your brother?" I managed to choke out bleakly. I was staring at Sister Maston's pretty face. How could Clyde Winston be related to such a human being?

"Yes, Crosby. And just between you and me, I think he's a little jealous of you and your girlfriend. What's her name? Is it Maria?"

"Maria," I whispered strickenly. "Her name is Maria Lopez." I was fuming. Clyde had a family? I avoided Clyde at school. The problem was that he found me no matter where I was. He'd waddle over and taunt and torment me, and then, from the little I could see through his greasy lensed glasses, he'd wink his reptilian eyes at me in a menacing way. Reform school was written all over him.

Sister Maston seemed very happy that there was a connection between Clyde and me. I didn't want to say too much. I was afraid I'd give away the truth about her dopey brother. I wondered fleetingly if she knew he was the worst bully on earth. So I smiled and said, "How is Clyde doing this year? We don't really talk that much."

"He's reading a little better," she said seriously. "It's always difficult for him, but I work with him when I can." She paused as though considering if she should say more. Evidently she thought she should, for now she asked me, "Crosby, how do sentences look when you read?"

I wanted to say sentences are beautiful and that I'd never met a sentence I didn't like, and if I did meet an unlikeable sentence, I'd fix it and make it better. And some sentences were so well put together that I memorized them after reading them once, they were so remarkably well written. But it would give away too much about me if I began to gush about sentences and books and reading.

So I said rather lamely, "I think sentences are nice, and I just read them and enjoy the story."

"Clyde reads some words backwards," Brenda said in a puzzled tone. "Sentences are lost on him. Sometimes he can read a word one second, but two second later, the same word throws him."

He most likely couldn't see the sentences to begin with, I was thinking. If he'd wipe off a few layers of grease from his glasses, he'd probably be a jim-dandy reader.

Brenda went on. "He's very hurt and self-conscious and sad about two things: his reading and his weight. My mother says he cries about those things every day when he comes home from school."

I was suddenly aware that I was learning far more than I wanted to, and I was beginning to regret that I had come with the Mastons. Clyde cried? Clyde self-conscious? There were probably two Clyde Winstons, because at school, the bully called Clyde revelled in his meanness. The one Brenda was describing must be an imposter.

I had to respond to Sister Maston, but how? And then my church-drenched upbringing came to my rescue. I croaked out a response that embraced everything and yet guaranteed nothing. "I'll pray for him," I uttered piously. And then in my mind, I prayed hastily, God bless Clyde the bully. I am nothing if not honest. I had kept my promise.

My words did the trick, for the Mastons seemed very happy at my religious remark.

A few minutes later we pulled into the Foster's Freeze parking lot. Brother Maston revved the Chevy's engine a couple of times before shutting it down. You can't exactly strut like a big shot when you use a crutch, but after getting out of a car like Brother Maston's, I tried to swagger a little, and at the same time, I was wondering why on earth I was bothering with one crutch. It had recently become unnecessary. Force of habit, I judged.

We approached the serving window. Foster's Freeze served soft ice cream. We had three large vanilla cones, the ice cream heaped up layer on swirling layer, which began to melt right away in the warm night air. We found a place at one of the outdoor benches and sat down.

While I worked on my cone, I thought about Clyde. I couldn't feel anything for Clyde—not pity or sorrow or kindness. He made his own bed, and now he had to sleep in it. The future for Clyde was certain. He'd end up at Velma's drinking and cussing and smoking and dancing and wasting his life. I had to settle it in my mind that the peopleness of people extended to a select group, and Clyde wasn't in it. You had to learn to help yourself if you wanted something good from life. Clyde upset my theory. I didn't want to acknowledge his peopleness. Clyde had a reading problem that made him sad and self-conscious? I didn't want to admit it to myself, but my legs and feet made my thoughts turn inward from time to time. Was that self-consciousness? Didn't those thoughts make me sad? But Clyde cried about the situation, and I was through with tears. I had the world of reading that kept me apart from crying. The heroes in my stories were bold and brave and above tears, and I wanted to be like them.

I suddenly wondered something about Clyde. Sister Maston was nearly done with her cone. I looked at her and said, "Does Clyde have a hobby?"

Sister Maston smiled. "Why, yes, Crosby. He does. He loves to fix things. He takes my mother's lamps apart and then puts them back together just to see how electricity works. He can wire and rewire anything. In fact, I never ask my husband to fix our toaster or our washing machine."

Brother Maston grinned. "Why should I. It's easier and faster to have Clyde do it. All I ever do is buy the parts."

You could have knocked me over with a feather. Clyde could do something useful for humanity? I could read books, and Clyde could wire things. It filled in a gap of sorts. Perhaps there was a trace of peopleness in Clyde, however slight, but dimly there.

We finished our ice cream, and Brother Maston said, "Let's take the scenic route home. What do you say, Crosby?"

I was game. "Sure, what do you have in mind?"

"I thought we'd take you home the back way on McClellan Road."

The back way home meant making a wide circle up in the foothills, following some winding roads in the process. Mom and Grandma didn't like the route because the roads were dark and narrow and dangerous. I didn't care. Brother Maston was driving. We got up from the bench and returned to the Chevy.

A few seconds later we left the Foster's Freeze parking lot and headed for the foothills. I kept looking out the window, hoping some of my classmates would see me cruising along in the hottest car around, but it was dark, and how could anybody see me? So I stopped waving out the window and sat back to enjoy the ride.

In the back of my mind now, there was a small, insistent thought nagging at me, but I couldn't bring it forward. But then two miles later, we turned onto Foothill Boulevard, and it finally hit me that just up ahead on McClellan Road, near a hairpin curve, there stood a dingy two-story yellow stucco building that I didn't want to see or have anything to do with.

Next to me, Sister Maston spoke up. "Isn't Velma's around here?"

And then sounding a little too casual, Brother Maston chimed in. "I think you're right, Bren," he said. "We'll be going by it in a second."

They were both right: Velma's was not only around here, it was also just ahead, for two blocks later, Brother Maston made a left onto McClellan Road and sure enough, there was Velma's Bar and Grille at the end of the block staring at me. I could see several small windows set in the dirty yellow stucco, two on either side of the front door—like cruel narrow eyes—and four on the second floor, where who knows what was going on. All the windows were dimly lit from within by a reddish glow. The front door was slightly ajar, apparently so the smoky interior of the place could air out.

Brother Maston had to slow down when he got closer to Velma's, because the road abruptly curved left directly in front of her establishment. I suddenly felt an unreasoning sense of sadness and anger and grief just by looking at the place.

The three of us in the car had just came from an evening in church, and no matter how you looked at it, we were superior in every way to the trashy patrons of Velma's Bar and Grille. The knowledge made me feel better. And for a second or two, I was hoping some poor, pathetic, useless human being would stumble out of Velma's door so I could get a good look at a specimen from the cesspool of humanity.

Brother Maston seemed to be driving a little slower than necessary as we cruised around the corner. I was staring intently at Velma's front door and the unpaved parking lot out front.

I heard Brother Maston take a deep breath. "Crosby," he said. "Can I ask you a question?"

"Sure," I said.

"Does this place look familiar to you?"

I told him I'd seen it a couple of times.

"No, Crosby. I mean the road here in front of Velma's, at this time of year, on a night just like this. Does any of this remind you of anything?"

I had learned over the last couple of years to deflect questions by asking a question. So now I asked blandly, "Why? Is it supposed to remind me of something?"

"Your Mom doesn't especially want anyone to remind you, Cros, but your father died not far from this spot."

He just said it right out loud. Not Pastor Barker, not Mom, not anyone at school had ever said this to me.

A little subdued and wary, I said sourly, "That's not news to me, but I don't have to think about it because if I do, it makes me mad at him, and at the funeral, Mom said he didn't know what he was doing, and I should forget all about it. And that's what you should do," I added sharply.

We now took the hairpin curve, and the road began to dip down toward a little creek. There was a narrow bridge over the creek, and as we crossed it, I could see the water flowing, black and shining and smooth in the moonlight.

"Thinking about it isn't wrong," Sister Maston said quietly, she had a kind voice that took me in and softened me up a little.

"A lot of worse things have happened to other people," I said, hoping to put an end to this line of thought. "People all over the world have terrible things that happen to them every day," I concluded carefully.

But the subject wouldn't go away, for now Brother Maston said, "Crosby, do you remember that you were with your father just before he died?"

I knew, but memory has its limits. If you fill your mind with fantastic thoughts all the time, you can push other things right out of your head because your mind is churning with other more compelling thoughts, like Dov Landau and Francie and Neely and Horatio Hornblower and Floral and Laurel and Zoral and Coral and the Joad family. I had a menagerie of characters to think about and dwell upon, and my father wasn't one of their number. I had a cabinet with ruined hinges where I could keep my characters safe and under my protection. They wouldn't come to harm under my care. They were safe in my heart.

I stared straight ahead. "I remember some of it," I said evasively. "But right now, I'm really tired and I have to go to school tomorrow, and if I don't get enough rest tonight, I won't be very alert tomorrow. My mother is very concerned about this." It was only a small speech, but it had the desired effect.

A rather subdued Brother Maston now said in a conciliating tone, "I didn't mean to bring up the past to hurt you, Crosby. But Bren is right: it isn't wrong to talk about what happened. My wife and I pray about a lot of things, and we mention you in prayer all the time."

I guessed it was Brother Maston's turn to make a speech. At any rate, the subject was now closed.

A few minutes later the Mastons pulled up in front of my house. I thanked them very kindly for the ice cream and got out. And as I watched them drive off, I was thinking about the useless crutch in my hand. My legs and feet hadn't bothered me for days. Over the last three years, my bones had mended and gained strength. I knew there was a moment where and when the crisis had occurred, and the pain and the damage had been inflicted. But most of the time, you don't have to think about something if you don't want to.

Mom had no doubt heard the rumble of the Chevy's Lake pipes, for she now opened the front door and asked me how everything went.

"It went great," I said. "I think from now on, I'll be going out every Sunday night." I grinned winningly. "That is—if it's okay with you."

Mom considered my proposal for a moment.

"We'll see about that," she said easily. It could have been worse. At least I hadn't been turned down flat.

It had been a long eventful day, beginning with Sunday school and church, and then one thing after another, till I ended up full of ice cream and a passenger in the hottest car in town, driving past Velma's Bar and Grille. I wasn't sure if there was a spare second in this day where I could have stuffed in one other event.

Ten minutes later, I plopped down wearily on my bed out on the back porch. Beatnik leaped up next to me and began to shove his large orange head against me.

"You tired too, boy?" I said. I held him and scratched behind his ragged ears.

Monte Vista catches a sort of on-again, off-again breeze from the San Francisco Bay. The windows in the back porch had screens, and I had learned which ones to open so that I could achieve a maximum flow of air because sometimes sweltering heat occurred in the summer. Sometimes I wondered what would happen if a violent wind came up and caused the windows to collapse inward with a great shattering of glass. I would be slashed by cruel shards raining down on me. There would be blood everywhere. Now there was a thought. Right now I needed to sleep, but thoughts of violence and my own blood filled my mind. I hated getting shots at the doctor's office, and I really hated the tiny spot of blood that appeared on my arm as a result. And no matter how it was explained or how a nurse might pat my skinny arm and assure me, I always laughed like a banshee when a needle pierced my skin. Even when I looked away, just the very thought of what was happening to me made me laugh. Human blood shedding is an awesome occurrence—the metallic taste and the sticky slick texture, and the crimson color and the pungent coppery smell. All of this seemed overlooked in my books. Some detectives blazed away with their .45s right into the bodies of crooks and thugs, and the detectives strolled casually away, because justice had been done to the bad guys.

But sudden death and blood splattering isn't exactly a walk in the park. I remembered when my class at school studied the Egyptians and how they mummified their own. I wondered what happened to the blood. Where does it all go when you die? I wondered about embalming and how many gallons of embalming fluid it would take to preserve one human being.

All in all, I concluded that the world sorely needed my message. Lying there in the stillness, on the edge of sleep. I thought about my contribution—people are in a predicament: death can take you before you breathe another breath, so you better be ready. The peopleness of people means there is hope, because God didn't make any trash when he made people. Therefore, if you see a bright flash in the sky, it may be that it is the dirty Commies dropping an atomic bomb, but you can at least hang on to the hope of Heaven when you duck and cover.

And with those thoughts, I dozed off into a peaceful, dreamless sleep.

* * * * *

-FRIDAY-

I woke up with the sun in my face, and the knowledge in my head that today was Friday. The week had gone just fine, except for two small incidents: first, yesterday, Clyde Winston had informed me that he was going to beat me to a pulp today. I guessed that his announcement was based on an imagined slight from me—yesterday I had told Clyde that he was probably going to enjoy prison food, and that when he was finally incarcerated, he should ask for an oversized bed in his cell, one with reinforced legs and industrial strength springs. Otherwise, when his bed collapsed, he'd be sleeping on the cold, hard concrete. Clyde didn't catch the humor at all. But the other kids in class laughed uproariously.

The second incident came from Grandma. She startled me with the news that Dad Upland was going to visit us on Saturday. I felt ambivalent about Dad's visit—was he going to whisk Grandma off and marry her somewhere or was he simply going to move in and then he and Grandma would take over the back porch? Where was I going to sleep? What about the cabinet with the ruined hinges? What if they moved in and wanted to store a few things on the shelves? And how was I going to tell Beatnik about the two intruders?

On the other hand, I mostly felt relief about Clyde's threat—at last I would exact my revenge. What Clyde didn't know was that I didn't need my crutch anymore. I had finally admitted to myself that I was using it out of habit, because people expected a hobbling Crosby, and if I didn't use it, I'd be barraged with questions, the worst of which would come from people at church. They'd say things like,

"So, you've had a miracle, Crosby? God has done a mighty act in your legs and feet, hasn't he, Crosby? Are you giving thanks for your new legs?" And so on.

My legs and feet weren't new. They were back to normal. It opened new vistas for me. My legs now supported me and carried me as they should. Clyde was in for a surprise today.

Our school cafeteria always served fish sticks on Fridays. Mom splurged a quarter just for me on Fridays because I craved fish sticks, which I would slather in tasty tartar sauce. So today, just before I left for school, Mom handed me a quarter and then gave me a frank, appraising look and said quite bluntly, "You know, Crosby, you could just leave that old crutch home today if you'd like."

She said that because I'd been showing off all week, coming to the dinner table without my crutch, and doing jumping jacks every evening and working in the yard a little.

I smiled. "I'll just use it today," I said easily. "I might need it." I didn't tell her why.

Grandma came up beside Mom. "You're a new boy, Crosby. It isn't just your legs that God has strengthened. Dad Upland told us three years ago that..." Grandma's voice trailed off.

Mom gave Grandma an exasperated look. "We agreed on this, Ma. And tomorrow is soon enough." She looked at me and said quickly, "Have a wonderful day, Crosby. We're going to miss you like crazy." She pinched my cheek. In her face was a shrewd, almost hard-boiled fondness. Then she gave me a little shove toward the front door.

I didn't exactly crave affection from Mom, but I was always hungry for her attention. She, more than any other, was the sounding board for all my ideas. She never grew tired of my thoughts, and even I knew that some of them were strange and unrealistic. But Mom always listened to me as though I were uttering brilliant and profound and fascinating truths.

I said I'd miss them too and went out the door. For a second or two, I wondered what Dad Upland had said three years ago, but at the moment, I had school and Maria and Clyde the bully on my mind, and so I didn't pursue the subject.

It was several blocks to school, and as long as no one could see me, I decided to simply walk and let the crutch hang on my arm by the loop that was situated midway between my elbow and wrist. I had lived with that loop and the handle farther down for three years. And today, I had decided it was its last day of use. However, I had already made up my mind that I needed it for one last purpose: Clyde Winston was going to taste metal today.

My cheek was still stinging from Mom's goodbye pinch. I thought about the look on her face when I left. It was typical of Mom to let me know she loved me without a flood of mushy words. She loved me in an astute and prudent sense. She gave me freedom and privacy. In return, I went to church and obeyed her on most occasions. Mom wasn't like her sisters. She was an interesting mixture of all their good features. She had Aunt Nelda's rather intense sense of duty, but Mom tempered it with a light touch that Aunt Nelda was lacking. I thought Aunt Nelda was a superb aunt even if she was somewhat humorless and occasionally ran roughshod over everyone within the sound of her voice.

Mom was fiercely practical about things. There were days when she went to work at Collier's Cannery, and I could see that she was tired. But there she was in the morning at the front door, a bag containing her rubber gloves, plastic apron, and lunch, hanging from her arm, ready to face another day's work. She'd give me a lion's growl and say, "We're going to fight the good fight today, Crosby!" She always included me in her adages about duty and work and living. Later when she came home, she'd tell me her dogs were tired and I'd bring her a cup of black coffee and we'd sit in the living room and I'd ask her questions about cannery work.

Mom had Aunt Violet's wry, gritty humor about life, but didn't share Aunt Violet's view about love and marriage and divorce. And Aunt Zonell's sensitive side showed in Mom, but neither Aunt Zonell's tragically broken heart, nor her inability to turn loose of the past found expression in Mom.

It was eerie how my Mom took the best from each of her sisters. She knew how to put the past in perspective without a sense of shame or a hint of self-pity. The fact was that I thought Mom had more shrewd common sense than most of the men I had ever known. Mom never dithered around or got flustered. She assessed a situation, made a decision, and then acted on it.

A mom like that is noticed. On the rare occasions when I had friends over to play, I usually lost them the second they walked in the door. They'd sit and talk to Mom. I didn't begrudge losing them. Mom was an expert listener, and I realized that my friends noticed her good sense and compassion like I did. So I would retire to the back porch and read and let my friends enjoy a few minutes with her.

I had walked three blocks by now without so much as a twinge of pain in my legs. By the time I passed San Fernando Street, I decided to play it safe, and so I began to sort of bounce my crutch along with me in a halfhearted way.

I realized now that I should have left it at home. Wasn't I Crosby the writer, the thinker, the protector of widows and orphans? Wasn't I now dry-eyed and tearless? Didn't I hold to the truth of the peopleness of people? So why was I holding on to a useless crutch? I wanted to live honestly and truthfully, and it suddenly seemed to me that I wasn't living by the writer's code. And I resolved right there to revive the Code of Chivalry too. That was two revivals: protecting widows and orphans and observing and recording all the many motions of life on paper.

I felt good about my resolutions. There now remained only one thing I needed to do in order to make the day complete, and that was to dispatch Clyde Winston the bully to the destiny he so richly deserved.

Lunch was when I knew Clyde would make his move. And sure enough, when Maria and I got in the lunch line, there he was just ahead of us. Presently he turned around and looked at us in a nasty way.

"Is that you, Crosby?" he said threateningly. "I hear you don't like to go near good, old Velma's. Maybe I could meet you there after school for a couple of beers."

No doubt about it, Clyde was gifted in the insult department. His comment almost threw me, but then I remembered that last Sunday night I had been a passenger in Brother Maston's Chevy and along with Sister Maston, the three of us had taken the scenic route home from Foster's Freeze. Probably Sister Maston had innocently mentioned that ride to her brother, which now gave him new resources with which to fashion insults.

"Clyde, could I speak with you on the playground right after lunch?" I asked politely.

"If you have something to say to me, you can say it now," he said sneeringly. "Or better yet, why don't you sing it to me, you singing pig." The other kids in line tittered with laughter.

"No, not now," I said calmly. "I want you to enjoy one last meal. What I have to say can wait."

Clyde blinked his eyes behind the greasy, thick lenses of his glasses. "Oh, aren't we funny," he said derisively.

Maria tugged at my sleeve. "Crosby, are you sure about this?" she said with real alarm in her voice. "This isn't like you."

I told her I was very sure. I hadn't said a word to Maria about what I intended to do to Clyde today, because I knew she would try and talk me out of it, and I wasn't about to let her do that. Nothing was going to weaken my resolve. A man had to know himself and be determined.

I didn't let Maria carry my lunch tray today although she had been in the habit of carrying it all year. Instead, I hung my crutch on my arm, picked up my tray, and strode firmly to a table. I then broke another precedent: I sat next to Maria. Several of our classmates were staring at us.

I understood why. In the past I had thought it was embarrassing to be seen with a girl, and even more embarrassing to let it be known that you liked her, but my world was changing around me. I had a grandmother who had suddenly become engaged to an old preacher. I was making real progress in my attempts at communicating with Abraham and Yetta Greenberg. I had legs and feet that were as good as new. I was determined more than ever to protect widows and orphans, and nothing was going to stop me from writing down stories about my intriguing relatives.

And there was one other change in my world: Maria. I now saw her in a different light. She was prettier than ever. Her long, shiny hair and radiant brown eyes and dark complexion spoke to me of exotic places and fascinating cultures. I had a lot to learn from my best friend.

Sitting next to me, Maria now said, "You've been different all week, Crosby. I'm not complaining about it, but you've changed."

"Different in what way?" I asked.

"You never argued in class, for one thing. And you've been so quiet. Why are you so different?"

Maria was being very tactful and kind. She hadn't mentioned the other change: I hadn't cried in class this week at all. So my plan had worked. I'd been as dry-eyed as a turnip all week.

There was someone else who was aware of the changes in me. I had noticed Teacher looking quizzically in my direction on several occasions this week as though she expected me to say something. A time or two I had been tempted to respond, but I always managed to hold my peace. And besides, I didn't appreciate it when people pressured me to feel something, whether it happened in church or school; I didn't like it at all. It was all a part of my experiment to find out what would happen if I kept quiet. All and all, I'd discovered that keeping my mouth shut and remaining dry-eyed had given me one of the best weeks I'd ever had. I think Teacher enjoyed it as well. Once this week, she'd even laughed out loud, and twice she'd smiled at us.

There was a question hanging in the air, and I needed to answer it.

"Maria, I am different," I began expansively. "And I hope it's for the good." I took a bite of fish stick, chewed it carefully, and swallowed. "I don't mind telling you that you have played a part in bringing about some of those changes."

Maria's pretty face went red and then a little redder. "Crosby," she said quite flustered, "you carry your own lunch tray and then sit with me, and now you say this!"

What power I had. Then I thought that maybe I'd gone too far, and I didn't want to leave the wrong impression. I wasn't proposing marriage after all.

I said hastily, "It's just that my life has been so weird lately. I'm realizing that it's up to me to dream and plan and work in order to bring about my own future." I dipped a fish stick in tartar sauce and took another bite. "I have three aunts, and you should hear them talk. They've had such interesting lives. When I was younger, I couldn't tell them apart, but now after hearing their stories, I couldn't mistake them for one another ever again. They're so unique. I bet each one of my aunts had dreams for the future when she was young, and when I listen to them now, I wonder if things could have turned out differently for them or if they'd even want things different."

I looked at Maria and shrugged. "Life is complicated, and it takes a lot of energy to figure it out, but you shouldn't let it get you down. In fact, my new motto is, 'Get ready for the future now!'"

Then all at once, I looked around and noticed that everyone at the table was silent and staring at me. I'd been talking a blue streak, and it was time to put a lid on it. I needed a good conclusion, so I added one more thought.

"If something terrible happens to you," I said thoughtfully, "then you should find a way out of it or through it and don't live like the past is an idol you're supposed to worship."

Then I grinned and extended a kind invitation to my fellow students. "You're all invited to the playground right after lunch," I said. "Clyde Winston and I will be a having a discussion."

Next to me, Maria said resignedly, "I'm going with you, but I'm not happy about it."

I nodded my head and then took our trays and walked over to the cafeteria worker who was in charge of scraping the leftover food off our trays into an overflowing garbage can. The trays were then placed on the racks in the large dishwashing machine. But since it was fish stick Friday, there was nothing to scrap off my tray; it had nearly been licked clean.

Once outside, we walked past our classroom and then out to the grass-covered playground. There was a small crowd already gathering on the field near one of the baseball backstops. I had my crutch with me, and now I flipped it over and gripped it by the tip. I stopped for a second and held it like a baseball bat over my shoulder. I took a few practice swings. Then I walked into the crowd.

Clyde was standing there, a big pimply grin on his face.

"Nice of you to show up, piggy boy," he said nastily. "What's it like to be covered with blood?"

"Yes, Clyde," I said patiently. "I know I was covered with blood in front of Velma's just before my father died." I stared at him. The crowd around us was very quiet.

Clyde's method was verbal torment, always followed by a wrestling match. Clyde didn't really use his fists, he generally threw his opponents to the ground and then sat on them. After that, his weight would squash the air out of their lungs, and they would give up immediately. Clyde was always the winner.

"You live a big fat stupid lie, because the principal went to every class and said no one should talk about what your father did, and so now little Crosby is so special and can't face the facts. And so everybody has to pretend that they don't know that your father tried to kill you. He was a drunk and a bum."

"You have several facts wrong," I said. "My father was a World War II veteran, and the war did something to him. And after the war, he drank. I don't understand it, but I know he was hurt and confused and angry and had nightmares. And alcohol didn't help him at all."

Clyde wasn't listening. He was busy working himself up and getting ready to make the usual dive at his opponent.

I held my crutch up by the tip in front of me. "If you try anything today, Clyde, I'm going to stop you with this." I lifted the crutch menacingly in front of his greasy nose.

"I don't want to hurt you, Clyde, but just about everything you say is so dumb that it makes me wonder why you don't wake up and come to church with your sister and get saved and sanctified and delivered. My pastor would be happy to pray for you and cast out all those demons."

Clyde spit out, "Church is for sissies."

I said reasonably, "I admit there was a time when I thought religion was only good for old ladies of both sexes, but I think differently now." I gave Clyde a winning smile. "What surprises me is that it took you three years to say the obvious. Why haven't you mentioned my father before? What took you so long, Clyde?"

"You talk too much, Mr. Brain," Clyde said sarcastically.

"Is that what's bothering you, that I get good grades?" I asked, a little astonished. Of course it was true. My entire study method was to read the chapter once. After that, there was no further need to review. If I required an answer when I was taking a test, I simply remembered what Teacher said or I recalled the page from the textbook and reread it in my mind till I came across the answer I was looking for. It was a simple method, really. My report cards were carbon copies of each other: All As and A+s.

Clyde now tried a new approach. "I don't think you've got the guts to use that thing on me," he said referring to the crutch. "I think you should go home to your momma and cry."

He was trying for the biggest insult he could find, I supposed. I remembered what Sister Maston told me about Clyde's reading problem and how he couldn't make out some words and how he sometimes read words backwards and how he often cried about it.

The bell was going to ring soon, and recess would end. I had to get to the bottom of this situation. The Clyde Winstons of this world are always full of themselves, predictable, boring, and quite tedious, and must be handled with kid gloves. This week, I had experimented with keeping quiet in class and talking frankly with Maria and facing a few facts about my father, and now it occurred to me that the experiments had yielded valuable information. Mostly, I had concluded that I liked change. One other experiment occurred to me now.

My crutch was still in my hand. I tossed it down on the ground. "On second thought," I said quietly, "why don't you use the crutch on me, Clyde? You can't do any worse damage to me than my father already did."

Clyde stared at me. Through his greasy glasses, I thought I saw bewildered eyes. A speechless Clyde was no Clyde at all. He was famous for his mouthiness, yet here he was, standing perfectly still, wordless and looking very confused. And there was my crutch on the ground within his reach.

"Go ahead, Clyde," I said softly. "No one will stop you. But I should remind you that blood is slippery, and you may have difficulty holding the crutch if your hands are covered in blood. The fact is that blood has a metallic taste and doesn't wash out of clothes so easily."

A few words burst out of Clyde's mouth. "Why did your father do what he did?" he said, still bewildered and staring as though the meaning of the taunts he had used on me had suddenly taken on flesh and blood.

"How do I know?" I asked shortly. "He died before I could ask him."

"When my father left us," Clyde said plaintively, "he just took off. Why didn't your dad just go away? He didn't have to hurt you."

"I didn't know your father was gone," I said genuinely surprised. It was a habit with me: whenever I found out that someone didn't have a father. I always wondered how it changed things. When my father died, Grandma came to live with Mom and me. As far as change goes, that was a good one.

"I think my dad used to drink with your dad," Clyde said, almost sounding human.

"Who didn't?" I said flatly. "He had lots of drinking buddies. You know what it was?" I was looking steadily at Clyde. He had lost his stance; he wasn't ready to pounce on me now.

"It was Velma's," I went on. "There's no worse place in town and no bigger collection of riffraff anywhere."

I turned around and looked at Maria, remembering that her father still visited Velma's place. I felt bad for him. Probably Mr. Lopez would come home someday and do something horrible to his family. Or maybe he wouldn't come home at all.

Clyde didn't pick up the crutch. Instead he looked around at the crowd of students and said sullenly, "I don't like this anymore."

For Clyde, this was a move toward sainthood. It seemed like he had actually realized a significant something and whatever it was had caused him to hesitate.

The bell rang, and the crowd began to break up. I looked at Clyde. He was just standing there, his expression sad and deflated. I suddenly thought of one last personal thing I wanted to say to him.

"Clyde, do you think you could take a look at my mother's vacuum cleaner? She's having real trouble getting it to work right."

Clyde looked up at me, clearly surprised and interested. "Why? What's wrong with it?"

We both started walking off the field, my crutch forgotten. We only had a minute or two to get back to the classroom.

"Clyde," I said patiently, "if I knew that I'd fix it. When she turns it on, the brushes don't rotate."

"The belt probably broke," Clyde said decisively. "I could fix that in a matter of seconds."

I told him my Mom had bought the vacuum at Sears, and Clyde said that brand was one of the easiest to fix. "Belts wear out all the time," he explained. "I try to keep a spare one at home just in case." He thought a minute. "The secret is you can't be afraid to get your hands dirty, and you have to have the right tools. If you want to fix something, you have to study it real close and then take it apart very carefully."

He told me another secret. "You should always lay out the parts you remove from whatever you're working on, piece by piece in perfect order, because then when you're done, everything will easily fit back together."

I told him I understood, but I still wanted him to fix it, because I wasn't that confident about taking things apart and then trying to put them back together, and if I watched him at work, maybe I could learn how to do it.

Clyde said he'd be glad to help, and we got back to class just before the late bell rang.

* * * * *

-SATURDAY-

The next morning I woke up wondering how much longer I would have the back porch to myself. It was only last Sunday morning that Grandma and Dad Upland had announced their engagement on my front porch. As far as I knew, they hadn't made any plans about their future except that Dad was coming over tonight. He probably wanted to size up the back porch and figure out a way to evict me and Beatnik from the premises.

I looked around me. Grandma's handmade quilts were on the beds, and the cabinet with the ruined hinges was off to my right. The washing machine and large sink were to my left near the kitchen door. Directly across from me, Beatnik was still sound asleep on his bed, his scruffy orange body tightly curled in on itself. The sun was shining through the windows on the side of the house which bordered on the orchard of prune trees. I knew the light from the sun would slowly spread its warmth throughout the porch as I applied myself to my usual Saturday morning devotional.

I crawled out of bed, got dressed in a white t-shirt, wash-faded jeans and a pair of well-broken-in sneakers, and then I carefully and quietly opened my cabinet of books. I noticed right away that two of the books, which I had left stacked up quite neatly in a corner, were not as I had left them. They were sticking out a little. I shoved them back in line, figuring that Grandma or Mom must have accidentally bumped into the cabinet, knocking the books out of place.

Then I grabbed two of my favorite books and gently closed the cabinet door. I sat down on the edge of my bed and began to read about serene Saturdays in Brooklyn. I wondered what it would be like to make my way around the neighborhood with a wagon, collecting rags which could be sold for a few cents to a rag dealer. And like the Nolans, I wanted to nail a coffee can to the floor in a closet for all my loose change, and then if there was an emergency, I'd have all that coffee can money at my fingertips. I thought about Mrs. Nolan's meatloaf made from stale bread and meat and chopped onions and spices, and then all mushed up together and baked to perfection. From time to time, I'd hinted to Mom that she ought to try out a new and interesting recipe that I'd read about. It was composed of two parts: first, Mrs. Nolan's meatloaf, and second, a topping of coffee and ketchup thickened by flour to be poured over the baked delicacy. But Mom was not impressed.

"Why, Crosby," she once told me, giving me a puzzled frown, "that kind of dish sounds like it's only for the poorest of the poor. We're on a tight budget, but not that tight!"

I relented a little after that. Still, the way the meatloaf was described in the book left my mouth watering and my stomach feeling deprived.

I put the Nolans aside, took up the other book, and began to read about the Rabinsky brothers, Jossi and Yakov, and how they had walked from their native Russia to Palestine around the turn of the century. They barely made it there, but they had determination and drive and nothing—not dangerous inhabitants of cities and villages along the route, not bitter weather, or gnawing hunger, or rugged, forbidding mountains—nothing could stop them. They worked jobs along the way. They spent time in jail, but when released always continued on their journey. The point was that they set out to walk to Palestine and that's what they did.

I liked stories about determined people. I sat there on my bed and remembered a few years ago when the television showed scenes of race riots in the city of Selma. At first, I thought the reporters were referring to the Selma I knew about, which was in the San Joaquin valley where Grandma's brother lived. His name was Stephen Plunk and he had a grape vineyard and all those reports about the violence in Selma frightened me. But then one day, Grandma told me about the two cities with the same name, and I felt much better, though I knew I would never forget the determined negroes in Alabama who wouldn't allow themselves to be shoved around. It was hard for me to imagine how they felt, being treated so badly. But I admired them for standing up to all those stupid hate-filled white bullies.

I had only had a small taste of that kind of treatment. Clyde Winston had shoved me around for a long time, but I finally stood up to him, and though I wouldn't exactly say I wanted him to win the school's big man on campus award, we were now at least communicating rather peacefully. I had finally admitted Clyde to the ranks of the peopleness of people, and he had never even been a candidate before yesterday. Yet there he was.

Beatnik, who hadn't moved since I began reading, now looked up at me and, instead of bounding over to my bed for a little scratching behind his ragged ears, jumped off his bed, crossed the room to the greenhouse door, and squeezed his body through the opening. He was undoubtedly on his way out to roam the neighborhood in search of food or romance or both. What a great life he lived.

I closed up my book and picked up the other I'd been reading and put them carefully back into the cabinet. I lined them all up straight and true and closed the doors.

I was feeling serene myself and not just because it was Saturday, but because of the changes that had taken place in my life recently. It seemed to me that if I could fix things up with Clyde Winston, and if I could face a few facts about my father's death, and if I could throw away a useless old crutch, then why should I be edgy and unsettled about a visit from Dad Upland? He probably didn't even know how I felt about the back porch. If I could speak to him privately, man to man, he'd come to understand the meaning of my living arrangements, which was simple: the back porch was mine. And Mom's and Grandma's mission in life was to take care of me. Other than that, Dad Upland was free to have his own living arrangements.

In the kitchen, I was prepared to bolt down a breakfast of eggs and bacon and toast and coffee. Grandma was already at the table, buttering toast for both of us, while Mom fried the eggs and bacon in the huge cast-iron skillet she'd used for every breakfast I could remember.

Grandma sipped at her coffee, gave Mom a peculiar sideways glance, and then looked at me.

"We'll be having company tonight," she said delicately.

"Yes, I know," I said evenly. "Dad Upland is going to be here."

"Brother and Sister Maston are coming also, Crosby," she added.

"The more the merrier," I said. Last Saturday night, my aunts had been here, and I was still happily remembering what I had heard then. Tonight sounded like another interesting occasion for more fascinating stories. Who knows what I would learn? I thought.

Mom came to the table now and scooped eggs and bacon out of the skillet onto my plate.

"Grandma and I are looking forward to a time of Christian fellowship too, Crosby," Mom said.

I was accustomed to the religious terminology Mom and Grandma used. It was my second language, and I was fluent in its use, though I rarely spoke it myself. It was Mom's habit to say things like "Christian fellowship," instead of "chitchat" or "chew the fat," and never "dish the dirt."

At any rate, with both Dad Upland and the Mastons here tonight, we were all going to end up sitting around and shooting the bull for hours.

When I finished breakfast, Mom said she wanted me to go to the store. This was a significant event for me. In the past, Mom walked to the store because I couldn't carry groceries and negotiate with my crutch at the same time, but now that the crutch was gone forever, I was ready for the task.

"We're having chicken fried round steak tonight, and I want you to pick out two good ones," Mom said. I was ready to eat right then. It was true that I wanted to try a stale bread meatloaf like Mrs. Nolan made, but chicken fried steak meant that I'd hear Mom pounding the steak with the edge of a plate to tenderize it, and then she'd coat it with flour and fry it to mouth-watering tastiness. When we had round steak for dinner, I ate like a wild man, consuming the fat and all.

Mom handed me a grocery list. I carefully checked it over. Then I went out the front door, crossed the empty lot, passed Skylar's Texaco on Steven's Creek Boulevard, and walked across Pasadena Avenue. I was now standing in front of Abraham and Yetta's variety store. I wanted to go in and talk to them both. Last week, Abraham and Yetta had talked to me more than they ever had, but now I resisted the impulse to visit them. Yet the fact was that they were two of the most engrossing people I knew, and I wanted to tell them about it. So I compromised. I told myself that when I went to their store for my next haircut, I'd engage them in another interesting conversation, but right now, I had the important responsibility of bringing home the groceries to Mom, including my choice of two tasty round steaks.

I crossed Steven's Creek Boulevard and entered Refredi's Market. I immediately made my way to the butcher's counter. There, behind the glass front, was a bountiful display of all kinds of meat, some of the cuts in shallow little white paper boats, and others cuts, including round steaks, spread out like a deck of cards, fanning off of each other in neat rows.

The butcher was Mr. Dennon. He had a shock of white hair and was very thick around the middle. He smiled constantly and always wore a red-stained apron. Mom had told me he had seven children. His family probably had free meat every day. I always thought if he were my father, I'd have round steak every meal.

Mr. Dennon now looked at me over the high counter and grinned. "Well, sir," he said heartily, "is that Crosby Hoggard, I see? Somebody told me you were walking again, and it looks like it's true. What can I do for you today?"

I told him I needed some round steaks and pointed to the ones I wanted. He tore off a sheet of butcher paper, laid it out on the counter, wrapped the meat up, sealed the package with a piece of brown tape, and crayoned the price on the outside.

I watched him rather absently. I was wondering who told him about me. I knew word would eventually get around that I didn't need my crutches anymore, but it seemed like word was flying around.

Mr. Dennon handed me my package, and I thanked him. Then I went to the front of the store and got a shopping cart. It only took me a few minutes to locate the other items on the grocery list and put them in the cart. I went back to the front of the store and got in line in one of the checkout lanes. I could hear other carts rolling into the line behind me. And then someone in back of me began to hum a rather tuneless melody. When I turned to see who it was, I was taken aback: it was Aunt Violet's husband, my Uncle Hamlin Vadney. And though I was looking right at him, it seemed as if he didn't know it was me. I wondered if he was shopping for Aunt Violet or if he'd just wandered off from home again. He didn't have any groceries with him.

"Uncle Hamlin? It's me, Crosby." He was looking right at me with no recognition in his eyes, but a second later, his face slowly lit up.

"I know who you are: Crosby. You're Opal's son." His voice was soft and deliberate. He stated each thought as though he had just discovered it at that moment, along with the words to convey it.

Uncle Hamlin was of medium height and very thin. He wore sneakers and Levis and a blue checkered shirt, one sleeve of which was rolled up above his elbow while the other was rolled down and buttoned at the wrist. His face wore an expression of mild amazement.

I held out my hand now. Uncle Hamlin looked at me for a puzzled second and then shook my hand. I knew that Uncle Hamlin had suffered a brain injury in World War II, but over the years, I had observed how Mom and Grandma treated him, so I just followed their example.

"I'm really glad to see you, Uncle Ham," I said truthfully. "Can I help you with anything?"

Uncle Hamlin's face saddened. "Your pa shouldn't have hurt his little boy," he said, shaking his head, his eyes welling up with tears. "I couldn't help," he said, "and I'm sorry for what he did to you." A few tears spilled down his cheeks.

Something caught at my throat. I could take this kind of talk from other people and show no emotion, but Uncle Hamlin was one of the purest and truest human beings I'd ever known. I didn't understand how he could get to me so easily.

I fought for a degree of self-control. "Let me pay for my groceries, and we'll talk about it outside, okay?"

Uncle Hamlin nodded and wiped at his cheeks with his palms.

Outside in the parking lot, I stood there holding a bag of groceries in one arm. I took hold of Uncle Ham's free hand and said, "Listen to me. You didn't do anything to be sorry for, and it wasn't your fault. What my father did is over and done with. So we both have to be strong. And besides," I said encouragingly, "that stuff all happened years ago, and have you noticed that I'm not using crutches anymore?" I turned loose of his hand and jumped up and down and spun around a few times.

"Do you remember when I had casts on both legs?" I went on. "And then the doctor made me wear those awful metal braces and then crutches and now look: nothing!"

Uncle Hamlin looked down at my legs. His face brightened immediately. "Your ma said you'd get better," he said, nodding his head slowly. "She told me and told me."

"Well," I said forcefully, "you're seeing it now, aren't you?"

I suddenly had a thought and then glanced around the parking lot. "Uncle Ham, where's Aunt Violet?"

Uncle Hamlin gave me a vague look. "I think she's at home," he said.

"Did you walk off and not tell her you were leaving?" I said matter-of-factly. "Because if you did, I could walk home with you."

Uncle Hamlin frowned as though in deep thought, and then he nodded emphatically. "She was busy in the backyard when I left. She had dirt all over her hands." He suddenly looked puzzled. And then he walked away without me.

I caught up to him in two strides, but he wasn't paying any attention to me. I had to get him home; it was my responsibility. So I tugged at his arm and said, "Uncle Ham, let's go this way."

But he pulled away from me and plunged off a few steps, like he was about to run. And at that moment, I noticed a car in the parking lot.

It was Maria's father's converted Chevy pickup. All his gardening tools were standing straight up and at attention in the pickup bed. Mr. Lopez was just getting out.

I called, "Mr. Lopez, are you busy? Could you help me for a minute? It's me Crosby Hoggard."

Mr. Lopez was out of his truck now, and when he saw me and Uncle Hamlin, he quickly came over to us.

"Sure, I know it's you, Crosby," Mr. Lopez said easily. "And I know Hambone too."

When Uncle Hamlin heard Mr. Lopez's voice, he stopped in his tracks and turned around with a huge grin on his face. "Is that you, Joey?"

I had never seen such a sudden transformation in my uncle. His face was relaxed and something like a strong confidence and familiarity spread across his features.

"It's Jose, man," Mr. Lopez said disgustedly. "Don't you ever get my name right?"

"I think he wandered off and ended up here," I said, lowering my voice. "I'm trying to get him back home."

Mr. Lopez said, "You don't have to whisper. Hambone knows where he is."

Uncle Hamlin said mischievously, "Violet's gonna be so mad at me."

"She's always mad," Mr. Lopez said cheerfully. "With a husband like you, I'm surprised she hasn't run away from home. You should be glad she still feeds you."

I was staring at Mr. Lopez. Mom and Grandma were normally very delicate around Uncle Hamlin, always speaking to him like he was a child, but Mr. Lopez needled my uncle with every word. And Uncle Hamlin seemed glad about it.

Mr. Lopez said, "I'll take you home, man." He led us to his truck. "Crosby, you can ride with us, and I'll take you home later." He looked at Uncle Hamlin. "Before I drop you off at home, let's go see if we can find a couple of cold brewskis, Hambone."

I started to say I had to get home immediately because the meat would spoil if I didn't get it refrigerated, but I didn't want to miss this. I wanted to ride in Mr. Lopez's truck, and I especially wanted to witness Aunt Violet's reaction when we brought Uncle Hamlin home.

Just like a real pickup truck, Mr. Lopez's modified Chevy only had a front seat, so I wound up sitting between Mr. Lopez and Uncle Hamlin. This was my second favorite car in the world. Brother Maston's 1955 Chevy held first place now and forever.

We pulled out of the parking lot, crossed Steven's Creek Boulevard, and headed down Pasadena Avenue.

Next to me, Uncle Hamlin suddenly said, "Crosby doesn't use his crutches anymore because God moves in mysterious ways when He's wondering what to do."

"That isn't what the old man said," Mr. Lopez pointed out. "He told us Crosby would walk to places that he couldn't imagine and say a bunch of words that God would teach him. And he'd stomp on the works of the devil."

"But we saved his life too," Uncle Hamlin said happily.

I was thinking, What old man? What places? Who saved what? And who was going to teach whom a bunch of words?

"Velma saved his life, and we watched," Mr. Lopez continued. "All we were doing was sitting inside her place, tipping back a few cold ones, and swapping lies about the war."

"You were the wire stringer, and I was the radio man," Uncle Hamlin said.

"You got that right, man," Mr. Lopez said. "Now be quiet, Hambone. I want to talk to Crosby."

Mr. Lopez made a right turn onto Lomita Avenue. "Maria said you talk about your accident now. Is that right?"

"I know how my father died," I said steadily. "And I know he tried to kill me. And it happened in front of Velma's Bar and Grille."

"You've come a long way, man," Mr. Lopez said. "You're like me and Hambone: a real veteran. We got purple hearts, but you got new legs."

That was news to me. "You were wounded in the war, Mr. Lopez?"

"I took a clean shot through the shoulder," he said. "And I bled a lot, but I was back in the field in three weeks."

"You had to carry the wire everywhere," Uncle Hamlin said to Mr. Lopez.

"That's right, man. I was a wire stringer on Guadalcanal, and I had to unreel copper telephone wire so the forward units could stay in communication with our rear base."

"I had it easy, though," Uncle Hamlin said. "I only walked close to the CO, and he used the phone on my back in Sicily. But then he blew up, and the radio blew up and cracked my head wide open. The medic took his shirt off and wrapped it around my skull because he was afraid of losing the pieces."

"And then you had surgery," I said. "And they put a stainless steel plate in your head."

Uncle Hamlin nodded. "That's the part I don't remember," he said firmly. "But the medic who saved my life came to see me later and told me all about it and said his name. Sometimes I can remember it." He suddenly snapped his fingers. "Oh yeah. His name was Lucas Jeffery Martin from Tulsa, Oklahoma. He sends me Christmas cards all the time."

"He sends you a Christmas card at Christmas, man," Mr. Lopez pointed out. "Not all the time."

"Because Christmas comes but once a year," Uncle Hamlin said helpfully. He rapped his skull with his knuckles. "Violet says I'm a real hardhead," he said with a huge grin.

Mr. Lopez had made a left on Orange Avenue and now he turned right on Alcazar Street. He pulled up in front of his tiny house. We climbed out of the truck.

"We got time for one beer, Hambone," Mr. Lopez said. "You guys wait here while I go in the house." He took my bag of groceries and pointed to the bench where I had sat last Sunday with Maria.

A few minutes later he came out of the house with two long-neck bottles of Pabst's Blue Ribbon beer and a Coca-Cola for me.

My mind was plunging around, sorting out details. Mr. Lopez and Uncle Hamlin knew each other, that was obvious. They had fought in different theaters of the war. It seemed like all my male relatives had been drafted. Uncle Floyd Purcell had served in the Pacific, and Uncle Hamlin in Sicily. And there were others. My father had been in the Philippines, but I didn't know much about that.

Then it occurred to me that I bore the wounds and scars from that night in front of Velma's, but they were of a different sort than those sustained in battle by Uncle Hamlin and Mr. Lopez. I was simply stomped on and run over by my own father. He had tried to kill me but was interrupted before he could finish me off.

I took a sip of my coke. And then Mr. Lopez said, "Rosa told me never bring company home while she's cleaning the house. So we can't go inside. But I told her I didn't know I was going to see you two today, so she just laughed and told me to go outside and talk to my friends."

Uncle Hamlin said gently, "You have a nice wife, Joey. Sometimes she gives me enchiladas."

"That's because you ask for them, Hambone. Man, you forget everything! It's a good thing you got a wife. She can do the remembering for you."

"We didn't have wives in the war, though," Uncle Hamlin said.

Mr. Lopez sighed. "A wife in the war," he said disgustedly. "We both got married later, man. I didn't even have a girlfriend when I was overseas." He shook his head. "I wasn't a letter writer like some of you guys, but if I'd had a wife, I'd of tried to write her."

Uncle Hamlin held his beer bottle up, looking through the brown glass. "Crosby should have a purple heart too," he said softly. "Tell Crosby about wire stringers, Joey."

Mr. Lopez said without irritation, "I already did." He looked at me and his brown-seamed face broke into a grin. "Your uncle thinks Joey is the same as Jose."

"What name did they call you by in the army?" I asked.

"Spic, mostly," Mr. Lopez said. "I got all the jobs nobody else wanted. When I wasn't rolling out telephone lines, they used me as a runner. About the time my company bivouacked for the night, some officer would yell for me by my other name, which was Pancho. I don't know why officers thought all Mexicans in the army were named Pancho, but that's what they called me. Can you believe that?"

he said ruefully. "Anyway, after I reported, they'd send me back to the rear for one thing or another."

"Why didn't they just use the phone?" I asked.

Mr. Lopez took a sip of beer. "Because they needed Pancho to pick up something somebody forgot."

"Like what?"

"A wallet or a bottle of whiskey or a deck of cards or a book or a magazine."

"When did you sleep?"

"Whenever I could," Mr. Lopez said with a shrug. "I was younger then. I didn't think about myself that much. I followed orders and kept my mouth shut. That way, I stayed out of trouble. They liked me too, because one time, one of my COs told me that if I wasn't a Spic, I could really go places in this man's army."

I was staring at Mr. Lopez. "Weren't you mad all the time? Didn't you hate the way they treated you?"

"I didn't feel much of anything in the war," Mr. Lopez said bluntly. "I wanted to do my duty and serve my country and then go home. Besides, it was a steady job, and I sent all my money home to my mother. And then she bought this house. She lived here till she died, and then it was mine."

"What about your father?" I asked.

"He lived with us for a while, and then he went back to Arizona. He never liked California. But that was a long time ago. I think he died a few years ago, but I'm not sure, because he never wrote us."

Uncle Hamlin yawned hugely and said, "And then you did yard work."

Mr. Lopez said, "We need to get Hambone home or he's going to take a siesta in my front yard." He shook his head wonderingly at Uncle Hamlin. "One beer is all it takes to make you sleepy, man."

I was through with my Coke. I set the bottle down on the bench. And then the front door opened, and Maria came out. Her soft hair shined around her pretty face. She was wearing a light-green dress and had a bottle of Coke in her hand.

Marie said, "Hello, Mr. Vadney. How are you?"

Uncle Hamlin grinned at Maria. "Your father is my best friend in the whole world," he said.

Maria knew my uncle? I was beginning to think I'd stayed to myself a little too much, and that I needed to get out more often. Uncle Hamlin seemed to be well known in the neighborhood.

Maria came over and sat next to me. "Papa, Crosby's crutches are gone," she said proudly.

"I can see that," Mr. Lopez said. "The old man said it would happen, and that we'd see with our own eyes what God would do."

I had heard enough. "What old man?" I demanded.

"The old man in the Chevy at Stella's. Me and Hambone were there, and the old man was a healer and a fortune teller." Mr. Lopez grew thoughtful. "I heard the sounds your bones made when the old man put his hands on your legs. It was like boards breaking and snapping, and I watched your legs straighten out when he took his hands away. And you were bleeding from your mouth and head, and your pants were soaked with blood, and I was feeling bad because I wasn't able to stop your dad from hurting you." He shook his head. "It was like a battlefield out there."

There was something I had to know. "What did Velma have to do with it?"

"She told your father to go home and tried to take you away from him," Mr. Lopez said. "She even called him a mean drunk, but that all happened before the old man showed up."

Maria wiped a tear away. I realized that a few more pieces of a three-year-old puzzle were now falling into place in my mind. My father took me to Velma's when he was already drunk. I hated the thought. Fathers weren't supposed to act like he did. My life was divided up between home, church, school, and books, and neither a violent father nor Velma's Bar and Grille were supposed to be part of it.

"I've said too much, Crosby," Mr. Lopez said. "But Velma was so angry that she knocked your dad in the head with a baseball bat when she saw what he was doing to you."

"And at one point that night, I was lying on the ground in front of Velma's," I said quietly, "and he was running over me with his car.

It was dark and there was dust everywhere and I was covered in a dirt and blood."

Mr. Lopez said, "And then right after your father drove away, your mom and the old man showed up."

"His name is Upland, Dad Upland we call him. And he's not a fortune-teller. He's a preacher. In my church, we call it prophesying. That's when God uses somebody to give a word from the Lord."

Mr. Lopez was holding the beer bottle tightly by the neck. He said reverently, "It was strange, but it got foggy right then, and after that, we saw the old man and your mom come through the fogbank, and me and Hambone moved aside. Velma was crying like a baby and holding you in her arms. Her dress had your blood all over it. The old man said, 'Thank you, dear woman,' to Velma and then your mom said, 'Pray for him right now, Dad!'"

Mr. Lopez paused for a second and then shook his head and continued in an amazed tone. "I've never heard a prayer like that. Velma was still holding you, and the old man put his hands on you and said, 'Father, grant a miracle to this boy!' Then the old man's voice sounded like one of my COs giving orders. He started commanding this and that."

I said, "What do you mean by 'this and that'?"

"He told the devil to take his filthy hands off of you and that your bones were going to be restored as good as new," he said in a bewildered tone. "I didn't know you could talk to bones and tell them what to do." Mr. Lopez set his bottle down. "Man," he said slowly, "that was something."

Uncle Hamlin spoke up. "Your mom prayed too. Only not like the old man. She told God he better get off his duff and go get a job."

Mr. Lopez turned and stared at my uncle. "Are you loco? That's what your wife tells you, Hambone. Don't you remember what Mrs. Hoggard said? She said, 'Make my son whole again, and I don't care if you do it now or later. Just heal him in Jesus' name!' And then just like that," Mr. Lopez added, snapping his fingers, "the fog went away."

Maria's eyes were glistening with tears, and Mr. Lopez was looking at me. I said, "I guess God thought it was best to fix me later, because now I'm doing great." I wanted to ask Mr. Lopez about the fog he saw, but before I could get the words out, Uncle Hamlin spoke up.

"When I went to Crosby's church," he said happily, "I got prayed for, and now I'm better too."

"I remember that, Uncle Ham," I said. "You used to whimper like a puppy all the time. Now you don't."

Uncle Hamlin nodded his head. "And I like to talk to Jesus because he never yells at me."

"What do you mean by that, Hambone?" Mr. Lopez demanded with a puzzled frown. "You mean my brother, Jesus? The one who lives in San Jose?"

"He's a good man like you, Joey." Uncle Hamlin said with a satisfied expression. "I get free enchiladas and beer from you and Jesus all the time."

We all shouted with laughter, including Uncle Hamlin.

Things broke up after that. Mr. Lopez and my uncle stood up and headed for the truck, and Maria went into the house and brought me the bag of groceries. When she handed me the bag, she said, "How can you be so brave, Crosby?"

"I didn't have much to do with it," I said. "The better question is, why me? Why not Uncle Hamlin? And what about my father?" I suddenly knew I'd said too much. Then I added, "I think I'm going to hear a lot more about it tonight."

I was only a seventh grader, but now I kissed Maria on the cheek. "I'll see you Monday, Maria. Let's talk at lunch, okay?"

And with a shy smile, Maria nodded her head.

I asked Maria if she was going to Sunday morning mass tomorrow, and she said that she and her parents always went to Saturday evening mass, because her father worked seven days a week during the summer months.

"Then you better burn a candle and say a prayer for me tonight," I said grimly. "I think some kind of trap is being planned for me, and I'm going to be ambushed by a gang of grownups tonight. The old man is coming over." Then I said through clenched teeth, "He might even be moving in."

And with that, I went out to the truck and resumed my place between Mr. Lopez and Uncle Hamlin.

Mr. Lopez backed out of his driveway, and five minutes later, we pulled up in front of Uncle Hamlin's house.

And just like Uncle Hamlin had said, Aunt Violet was out in the backyard working with her flowers. And to my chagrin, it turned out that she'd sent Uncle Hamlin to Refredi's with a list of things to buy. I had jumped to the conclusion that he'd wandered off.

"It doesn't matter, Crosby," Aunt Violet told me with a chuckle. "I'll take care of the shopping later." She turned to Mr. Lopez. "Thanks for bringing him home, Jose," she said kindly.

I told Mr. Lopez I wanted to walk the rest of the way home, and he drove off. I needed to walk home because it would give me a few minutes to think about the events of the past few days. I had learned a pile of details and I wanted to sort them out.

In a strange way, from several directions, I was catching up on the missing scenes of my own life. Even Clyde Winston knew some of the details that I'd shoved aside, because he'd told me yesterday that my father had tried to kill me. And Mr. Lopez and Uncle Hamlin had been there at Velma's and witnessed it all. So, I was the object of an unsolicited miracle—I hadn't asked for one. Dad Upland was responsible for that. I admitted to myself that I was fascinated by the facts surrounding what had happened, but I didn't especially enjoy being the center of events.

Or was I the center? Mr. Lopez had said that Velma had saved my life while others watched. I had no image of Velma to anchor my mind to. There was no face there. I didn't know if Velma was young or old or bald or blind.

I was near home now. I shifted the bag of groceries to the other arm and asked myself, how on earth had Mom come to be at Velma's? And what about Dad Upland? He was there? Then with a sadness that nearly choked me, I wondered about my father dying later that night. Every once in a while, the name Jeff Hoggard invaded and tormented my mind, but I never wanted to say it out loud, because the man behind the name had hurt my mother and tried to destroy me.

Sometimes in school, I was required to fill out forms which had a line where I was supposed to write down information about my father. I always wrote the word *deceased*. I had worked hard memorizing the spelling of that word. I had come to depend on it to stave off questions, because we not only had occasional forms to fill out, but also, from time to time, we were asked in class about our fathers. I always carefully and quietly muttered my memorized word, and then I'd watch Teacher's reaction. Most of the time, there was a stunned face and a little hesitation before Teacher would move on to the next student.

I sometimes wondered about hell. I could easily frame an image of hell in my mind. That wasn't difficult to do. It was referred to in many of Pastor Barker's sermons. It was unquenchable fire and flames, and it was eternal. All sinners went there, and there was no escape.

So the problem now was this: Mr. Lopez had said that Dad Upland had prayed that I would have a miracle, and I supposed that was accurate. I was walking perfectly after years of being crippled up. But if one miracle was possible, why not two? Why hadn't Dad asked for more? Like one for my father? I remembered so little about his life, and it didn't seem right that now I had to think about him in hell.

Pastor Barker said memories of this life persisted in hell, and he always sounded congenial and satisfied when he said it. In fact, Pastor Barker seemed like he was anxious to kick people in the seat of their pants so they could get into the flames quickly and efficiently. Once in a while, I wondered if Pastor Barker ever thought anything through. It seemed to me that he should talk about hell with a tear in his eye.

Furthermore, if Pastor Barker had something important to say about eternal destinies, how in the blazes did he not know that he should dwell on telling people how to get to Heaven? I was going to have to talk to him about this someday.

When I got home, I could hear Mom in the kitchen. I went in and set the bag of groceries on the kitchen table and then told her about what had happened at Refredi's. She seemed satisfied and happy.

"I'm glad you were there, Crosby," she said. "I'm sure Uncle Hamlin was well taken care of if you were with him."

I felt genuinely proud. Mom's words gave me a certain confidence that I couldn't find anywhere else. I didn't say anything to her about Velma's or what Mr. Lopez had told me. There would be time enough for that later.

The Mastons arrived first for what was about to become a cool evening. The bay breeze had started up and was just now blowing in when I distinctly heard the mellow rumble from the twin Lake pipes of Brother Maston's Chevy. And when he pulled up in front, he deliberately revved the engine a couple of times, no doubt for my benefit, and then shut the engine off, the sound from the pipes echoing smoothly away into the evening air.

At the door, Brother Maston and Brenda greeted Mom and Grandma with the usual bear hugs. Then Brother Maston said, "Sister Opal, you look as young as ever."

Grandma said, "And do I look as old as ever?" She had her hands on her hips and a teasing challenge in her voice.

"You're the source of all the family beauty, Sister Plunk," Brother Maston said stoutly. He bowed deeply from the waist. "I'm humbled to be here."

Sister Maston smiled at me. "Crosby, I believe you're getting taller every day."

There were more pleasantries, but I wasn't listening to them. I had decided that if the evening's theme was to be all about Crosby Hoggard and what had happened to him three years ago when his father tried to kill him, that I was greatly outnumbered. My suspicion was that relatives and friends nearest me were worried that I would have big mental problems if I wasn't told the truth, and the sooner the better.

It was the part about being outnumbered and outgunned that bothered me the most. On one side, there was Mom, Grandma, Brother and Sister Maston, along with Dad Upland; and on the other side was me. In other words, the odds were stacked against me.

I am nothing if not perceptive. In order to make the most of the evening, I had a few tricks up my sleeve; outnumbered or not, I was going to assert myself and stake out my territory.

Of course, things could get a little sticky tonight, especially if Dad felt like prophesying again or Mom and Grandma turned on the waterworks. But it seemed to me that if Jody could shoot Flag and if the Joads could just pack up and leave Oklahoma behind and head out for California on Route 66, and if Francie and Neeley could go forward with their lives after the death of their father, then I could face my own life and destiny and not allow anyone to tell me what to do. I was the only one living in my skin, and I had free will and conscience like everybody else. Who then was granted the authority to know me better than I knew myself? After all, in the last three years, I had achieved a deep and profound self-knowledge through a disciplined program of extensive and unceasing reading of the greatest novels I could lay my hands on. All the stories were filled with daring, iron-hearted, rugged characters who, against all the odds, had carved out magnificent lives for themselves.

And so now I thought about Dov Landau and how he had survived Auschwitz. No matter what tonight held, I was determined to survive. I didn't want to be humanly lectured or divinely manipulated as though—now that I supposedly had a God-given gradual miracle—I was obligated out of a profound sense of gratitude to be a cardboard cutout follower of a religious destiny. I wanted a hand in determining my own destiny. The real Crosby couldn't be confined in a narrow religious life. I was a complex human being, and my three-year-reading jag had opened my eyes to amazing possibilities. I determined that tonight I would be agreeable and pleasant and cooly alert to what was said.

And there was one other thing. How was I supposed to know for sure that I had experienced a miracle? What had happened to me and my legs and feet probably would have happened to me anyway. Or maybe it was the science of medicine, and I'd been treated by brilliant doctors who knew just what to do for me. Or maybe I was subject to religious delusions or the power of influence. At any rate, no matter what, tonight, I was going to be on guard.

Mom had everybody sit in the living room, and she and Grandma served us iced tea.

Then a few minutes past six, Dad Upland drove up in his old Chevrolet. I could see him out the front window. It took Dad a while just to open the door and climb out. I decided to initiate contact with him, and so I got up, pushed open the screen door, and walked out to the front gate.

Dad came around to the back of his car and then saw me. I walked over to him and shook his hand.

"Good evening, Reverend Upland," I said quite calmly and formally. His eighty-five years showed more than they did last Sunday. He seemed thinner, even haggard. His white hair was neatly combed, and his eyebrows were still in a mad tangle over his sky-blue eyes. He was wearing the same gray suit as last Sunday.

And then I asked myself, where had he been all week? Wasn't he engaged to my grandmother? As far as I knew, there hadn't been so much as a single phone call from him to Grandma in the past week. Several times I had wondered if I'd dreamed the whole thing.

Dad halted and stared quite frankly at me. "You are walking, and you have no fear," he said finally.

Before he could go on, I abruptly asked Dad if he'd like to see the prune trees alongside the house.

"They're amazing trees," I said. "The fruit isn't ripe yet, but I like to think of the trees as if they were gnarled old soldiers on guard duty, protecting our house. I know each tree like it was a real person," I babbled rather absurdly. I had never spoken this thought to anyone, and now I had just blurted it out.

Dad wasn't surprised or shocked by my words. We walked the few steps over to the edge of the orchard, and I pointed to one of the trees.

"I think this one is dying," I said. "Last year, it bore almost no fruit, and this year, as you can see, there aren't even a dozen leaves on it."

Dad watched me when I spoke. He said, "It's a sad thing that an orchard isn't cared for. It's even sadder that people are overlooked and ignored and considered unimportant."

The bay breeze was cooling things off now. The sun wouldn't go down for another hour or two. Overall, the orchard was a good place to be.

"I wanted to say thanks for helping me when you did," I said.

"I didn't do much," Dad said simply. "I was just following orders."

I walked over to the nearest tree and pulled off a small piece of bark. It was dark brown, as hard as stone, and as light as a blade of grass.

Dad followed me and said quietly, "I won't soon forget that evening, young man."

"I know exactly what happened," I said quickly. I thought I might as well try my first trick, the point of which was to take the wind out of his old sails.

If there were things to be revealed tonight, they would come from me. "My Dad took me to Velma's after he argued with my Mom. My Dad was a mean drunk, and he had come home drunk that night. And when you're a mean drunk, you get filled with fears and anger and self-hatred. My Mom had never even said 'boo' to my Dad about his drinking, but he didn't understand her devotion. He feared her kind of love and compassion, and he couldn't think straight when he was drinking. So he hit her, but she wouldn't tell anyone. I heard it and saw it when I was growing up. And every Sunday night when my Mom and I went to church, my father went to Velma's and drank."

I paused and tossed the little piece of bark I was holding at the nearest tree. "Sometimes he wouldn't come home for days," I went on. "And some paydays he'd gamble his entire week's pay away, but my Mom wouldn't give up on him. She never stopped praying for him."

I gave Dad Upland a steady look. "You were preaching that night," I suddenly remembered. "And when my Mom and I were getting ready for church, my Dad left the house. But he must have gone to Velma's and slugged down a fifth of whiskey in five minutes, because he came home just as Mom and I were leaving. He grabbed me and threw me in the car, and Mom said, 'Oh, Jeff, not little Crosby!' Then my Dad said, 'I'll be at Velma's,' and then drove off."

I swallowed hard and continued. "But when we got to Velma's, she confronted my Dad in the doorway. My Dad had me by the hand, and Velma told him don't be a mean drunk, and she said he had a nice wife and he should go home and sleep it off. Then she reached for me and said she'd see that I'd get home safely. But my Dad grabbed me up in his arms and ran back to his car and threw me in and slammed the door shut. He was standing by the driver's door when Mr. Lopez and my Uncle Hamlin came outside and tried to talk to him, but nobody could make him listen."

With his head bowed, Dad Upland was listening intently to my every word, and I was feeling like someone was dropping entire sentences into my mind.

"I remember he smelled like whiskey," I went on, "and I hated that smell. Mr. Lopez managed to lunge for the door and get it open, but when he reached for the car keys, my Dad hit him, and Mr. Lopez fell against the car and slid to the ground."

The next thing I said made my eyes sting with tears. "Then my Uncle Hamlin Vadney came over and said, 'It's me, Jeff. It's Hambone.' But my Dad called him a crazy, ignorant fool and shoved him away."

I didn't like this story at all. I was telling it only because I wanted to go back into the house and announce to Mom and Grandma and Brother and Sister Maston that Dad Upland and I had discussed the past and now like one of those half-hour cowboy television shows, everything was neatly resolved, and we could forget all about it and never speak of the past again. All the loose ends were accounted for, and Crosby was completely informed and beautifully adjusted to all the facts.

I wasn't going to be like Aunt Zonell, chained to Arthur Potter and the past. And I wasn't going to have a permanent broken heart either.

I held my hand up to Dad Upland. "I know you as a preacher want to speak, but as I said, I know all about what really happened.

I've been doing a lot of remembering this week, and it's all very clear to me now."

So I continued. "I managed to open my door and crawl out of the car. When my Dad saw me, he said, 'I'll teach you to try and get away!' Then everything happened faster than I can tell it. My Dad picked me up by one arm and threw me down, and then he started stomping on me. I tried to curl up in a ball and make a smaller target, but he kept stomping. I was crying and screaming for him to stop. That was when Mr. Lopez and my Uncle Hamlin came around the back of the car and tried to stop him, but my Dad was insane with rage. In two seconds, he laid them both out on the ground with his fists, which gave me time to crawl under the car. My Dad got down on his hands and knees and began to grab for me, but I scooted back by the rear wheels. Then he got up and ran around to the driver's side and got in the car. When he put the car into reverse, he backed up over my legs. I tried to drag myself out of the way as fast as I could, but he got me again when he pulled forward."

I took a deep breath. "Velma had gone into the bar and came out with a baseball bat. Mr. Lopez and my uncle were back on their feet by this time and were beating on the car and trying to get to my Dad, but he'd locked all the doors. Velma just walked over and broke his window with one blow, and then she swung the bat and clipped my Dad in the head. The sound was like swinging the bat against a tree trunk.

"I was lying on the ground and smelling the whiskey smell and the dust and my own blood. I wanted to say something, but mostly, all I could do was spit up blood. My legs were numb and twisted and turned. When my Dad backed up over me, the tires had mangled the cloth of my church pants and torn them, and I remember thinking that Mom was going to have a lot of cleaning and sewing to do.

"When Velma hit Dad, he reversed the car again, and this time he ran over my feet. I heard them make a snapping, crunching sound, and I saw them flatten out in front of my eyes. But the pain seemed distant, and all I could think about was how Mom was going to feel when she saw me, and I didn't want her to feel sad.

"My father just kept backing up after that, and when he was a long way off, he turned the car around and sped away, and I never saw him again."

Dad Upland nodded his head. "What happened was your Mom came to the church and said, 'Come quick, Jeff's got Crosby.'"

"I know," I said hurriedly. "She interrupted the Sunday night service." I was nodding rapidly.

Dad Upland cut in. "That was when Pastor Barker told everyone to pray, and then I left the building because I knew I had to get to Velma's."

I continued the story. "And when you got there, I was lying on the ground and bleeding a lot and still conscious, and Velma had used her finger to pull my tongue out of the back of my throat so I wouldn't choke to death." I hesitated for one stricken moment, feeling completely guilty and ashamed. Then I continued, nearly whispering. "Velma was holding me in her arms and crying and saying, 'You darlin' little boy. If you were mine, I'd take real good care of you, honey, but the TB got my own boy and took him away. You sweet little guy, just keep looking at me. Your Pa ain't gonna hurt you no more. Velma's gonna take care of you. You're gonna be okay.'

"I couldn't feel my feet or legs, but I still remember feeling Velma's tears falling warm and soft on my face. Her voice was like my mother's. Velma saved my life because the shock from my injuries and the loss of blood should have killed me, but Velma kept me awake and focused."

And then, all at once, I didn't want to talk anymore. The topic was emotionally exhausting. Besides, I was confident that I had covered all the significant details. I thought what I needed to do now was to somehow get Dad into the house, and then Mom or Grandma could talk to him. I had done my part.

Then I smelled the aroma of steak cooking. I turned around and looked at the house. Mom was frying the floured steaks in the big cast-iron skillet. And suddenly, I was ravenously hungry.

I gave Dad Upland a wary look and said hastily, "And then you laid your hands on me and said a few words about me and I got better, and now I'm doing great," I concluded brightly. I jumped up and down and ran in place to demonstrate the truthfulness of my words.

"You have most of the story correct," Dad informed me, taking me by the hand. I couldn't tell if he was holding my hand to steady himself or if he just wanted me to point him in the right direction.

We began to walk toward the house. "Where have you been this week," I asked conversationally.

"Fasting and praying," Dad said. "I knew this week would be filled with a heavy responsibility, and I wanted to be prepared."

"You haven't eaten anything all week?" I was amazed.

"Today is the day I decided to break my fast," Dad said. Then he suddenly halted and, still holding my hand, looked in my eyes and said, "I feel it is important to tell you that some of the details you left out are difficult to talk about. I've never mentioned what occurred that night to anyone, and I've never used your story as an illustration."

Dad Upland was making an extraordinary admission. Preachers were notorious for their lack of any sense of confidentiality. If you were so unfortunate as to whisper a family secret in confidence to any preacher I ever knew, you could count on your secret, including names and dates and locations, being used as a sermon illustration the next Sunday. We had essentially gotten rid of all gossip in my church; you could learn everything you wanted to know by listening carefully to Pastor's sermon illustrations and then putting two and two together for yourself.

And yet here was Dad Upland promising that he'd never mentioned the events of that Sunday night to anyone, clear evidence that the age of miracles had not passed.

As usual, we ate in the kitchen around the big table. Mom had closed the kitchen door because the June weather had cooled off, and with the bay breeze, it could become quite chilly even this time of year.

So far this evening, I had come up with two tricks that I thought would control the flow of information: first, tell Dad Upland all about that Sunday night myself so that no one could add anything later, and the second trick was to tell everyone around the table that Dad and I had just had a powerful exchange of facts so that there was no need for further details from anyone because that would be redundant, and there were plenty of other things to talk about.

I felt as though I had been only partially effective so far. The breakdown was within me. When I was standing among my prune trees, many details had come back to me, accompanied by sudden flashing images emblazoned across my mind. The past, which I was trying to dispose of, had a way of intriguing me. What other facts from that night needed to be told, so much so that Dad Upland had to fast and pray to tell them?

A few minutes later, true to form, my plate was heaped with chicken fried steak, mashed potatoes, spinach, and corn on the cob, and all of it smothered in a half inch of steak gravy. I was thinking about last Sunday at this same table and how my plate was also overflowing then. I remembered someone getting kicked under the table that day, and Mom admonishing Brother Maston later when he brought up a prophecy that he said was well known. I had missed several signals that day. I figured that last Sunday's signals had probably centered on deciding the right time to tell Crosby about the past, which was now inexorably making itself known.

I took the bull by the horns and now utilized trick number two. "Reverend Upland and I were outside a few minutes ago clarifying several details about the Sunday night when I was injured. We basically went over every detail and discussed everyone who was there and the role each person played in saving my life." I wiped a hand across my brow and then flicked off the imaginary sweat. "And what a story it is!" I said dramatically. "And now that I've heard it all, why don't we drop the subject, eat a hearty meal, and enjoy an evening of Christian fellowship."

I quickly loaded my fork with steak fat and mashed potatoes and gravy and shoved it all into my mouth. I chewed and chewed and swallowed and smiled.

But then Brother Maston spoke up. "I was there too, Crosby," he said. "I heard the whole thing."

I slammed my fork down. "No, I don't think you were," I said sharply. "I never saw you and therefore you weren't there. It's all logical and consistent."

"Of course you never saw me, and I never saw you," Brother Maston said calmly. "Not until the cloud lifted."

I remembered the fog. It seemed unusual to have fog form in that little area in front of Velma's, but then again, California has unusual weather patterns.

Dad Upland said quietly, "I can't say that I've ever seen anything like it before."

"You've never seen fog before?" I asked incredulously.

"It wasn't fog, Crosby," Brother Maston said firmly. He paused. "I need to start at the beginning. First of all, everybody knew your Dad hung out at Velma's, so when your Mom came into the church that night and said, 'Come quick. Jeff's got Crosby,' I knew where he had you. I told the people around me to get your Mom and Dad Upland out to my car. I knew nobody could get them to Velma's as fast as I could. Before I reached the church doors, I heard Pastor Barker telling everyone to start praying.

"Once outside, I flung the car doors open and then ran around to the driver's side and hopped in. For an old guy, Dad Upland was moving pretty fast. The two of them got in the car, and I pulled out of the lot before your Mom's door was closed. When we pulled up in front of Velma's, it was just minutes after your father had left."

Brother Maston paused again and then went on, his voice tightly controlled. "I saw what I thought was fog, but when I tried to get to you, I couldn't. Only Reverend Upland and your Mom got through."

"Why didn't you get through? What in the world are you talking about?" I felt a churning in my stomach. A sense of alarm welled up in me. I bit my lower lip and waited.

"I'm saying I bounced off the fog," Brother Maston said. "That's why I said I heard the whole thing because I couldn't see anything."

I had heard enough. "I don't believe you!" I said furiously. I stood up. "I've heard about religious delusions and bleeding pictures of Jesus and crying pictures of Mary and glory clouds forming, but enough is enough!"

I was breathing rapidly, and now I grabbed another breath and said heatedly, "I'm not the center! I'm not special. Why would God go to all that trouble for one useless twelve-year-old boy? I'm nothing but a big fat sinner who deserves hell. If God wants to do something with a kid, He should pick a kid He can trust. I sin all the time! In fact, I read dirty novels, and they're filled with swear words and filth and smut and violence. Maria should hear from God and have a miracle because she has to put up with me, and she's brave, and God could really use her."

No one was eating now. Every eye was on me. I pointed at Dad Upland. "You prayed for me, but Velma saved my life. She put her bony old finger in my mouth and flipped my tongue back where it was supposed to be so I wouldn't choke to death."

It had been a week of remembering. And then another fact hit me like a blow in the stomach. I said abruptly, "Velma died a few weeks later."

I sat down and stared at my plate. "How did I get so confused about Velma?" I said miserably. "She wasn't the enemy, she was a saint. She was fearless and courageous and loving. How did I ever get the impression that she was evil?"

I looked at Mom. "You thanked her for saving my life that night, because I remember watching the two of you hugging when they put me into the ambulance."

Mom nodded, brushing a tear away. "Velma was a veteran of World War II. She drove generals around in Europe. She was as tough as nails and had a great big soft heart. She wanted to come to the hospital with me, but I told her I'd take care of it."

I said, "You stayed all night with me at O'Connor's Hospital in San Jose."

"And while the doctors were checking you over, a policeman found me in the hospital waiting room and gave me your father's wallet. Then he told me that Jeff had crashed his car into a tree and died."

I shook my head wonderingly and asked my Mom, "How could you be so strong? Why didn't you get mad at God and tell him off?"

"That's easy to answer," Mom said. "Because I couldn't have made it through it all without him."

I had never considered that. The knowledge of what had happened that night had always filtered through what I thought about it; I had never considered what Mom had endured that night at Velma's and at the hospital.

I wanted to wrap things up. So I told everyone what I could remember about the next few days, how the doctors had x-rayed me, put casts on my legs and feet, and how I had used crutches so I could attend my Dad's funeral.

I looked at Mom. "We went to two funerals that month, one for my father and the other for Velma a few weeks later."

I remembered more about Velma's funeral than my Dad's funeral. Velma was Catholic, and the priest at her funeral was wearing a black robe that reminded me of Zorro's cape. I couldn't recall anything anybody had said during the ceremony, because all I could think about was the priest suddenly snapping his whip around one of the rafters, swinging out a window, and landing in the saddle of his waiting stallion.

Then Mom told me two things I didn't know. "Velma was dying of cancer when she saved your life. And even though her doctors warned her not to, she stubbornly hung on to her daily work routine up to the last moment." Mom slowly shook her head. "Velma was an amazing woman. And by the way, Crosby, she paid all your doctor bills."

Everyone was quiet around the table, our meal forgotten. Brother Maston was holding his wife's hand, and Grandma, for some reason, was giving Dad Upland a wide-eyed, inquiring look. Mom looked relieved, as though a great weight had been lifted off her shoulders.

Grandma spoke up rather impatiently. "Tell him the prophecy, Dad. What are you waiting for?"

I jumped in at that point. "A prophecy?" I said, almost contemptuously. "What about what I just said? I don't believe God does things like snapping bones back into place and fixing feet and ankles and legs for a worthless sinner like me."

Dad Upland's mind seemed to jump a little. "It's so," he said thoughtfully, "that God uses me in unusual ways. I recollect, young man, that God gave me a word for you, and it was a message that was unusual to my experience."

Our food was sitting unnoticed on our plates. I hated to see a good meal ignored, so I picked up my fork and began to eat. I had a third trick in mind: utter indifference—I would feign attentiveness, display an expression of sincere and concentrated interest, but underneath everything, I would be distant, aloof, and cynically calculating.

I took another bite and then noticed that I was the only one eating. So I took another mouthful, chewed, and swallowed. I was trying to prime the pump, but nobody was taking the hint. I put my fork down again, only this time with a bang. And despite all my firm resolutions and subtle tricks, and with a barely concealed sense of dread, I said a little too loudly, "All right! I'm ready. What did God say about me?"

Dad Upland's face wrinkled up into a wide grin. "You can't force God to speak, but I'll say this: when I got into Brother Maston's car that night, He did speak to me. The Lord told me clearly, 'If you'll trust me, I'll show you my glory.' So I just sat back and enjoyed the ride to Velma's, because I wanted to see what God was going to do."

Dad continued, his thoughts seeming jumpy and jumbled to me. "Now I've had words from the Lord before, but there was a unique thing about that night because I had a vision and a word from the Lord. He told me to deliver a prophecy, but hold on to the vision. I was surprised by the vision. I saw a young man lifting people and holding them up. I have learned that when God gives you a vision, He sometimes wants you to meditate on the meaning. And in the vision, I saw the young man preaching, and then the people shouted with laughter and were filled with joy, and they were unafraid and began to dance.

I was staring at Dad, wondering why he wasn't getting to the point. "Vision, Schmizon," I muttered sullenly. "I hate dancing."

Dad ignored my comment and went on. "The Lord said, 'This generation has a work to do!' I was frankly confused at what I'd heard. Then I realized that God was speaking to a generation through that young man. God had joy in store for them. He loved them all and wanted to save them and give them power to serve him."

"But what did God say about me?" I demanded heavily. My anguish was real.

"Oh, it including you, all right," Dad said pleasantly enough. "In fact, for a long time I thought you were the young man in the vision. Then I realized that only one Man can hold us human beings up and help us."

I confess I felt relieved. I wasn't the center, and I didn't want to be. Dad's vision, whatever it meant, included me, but didn't isolate me either. I had company.

Grandma broke in and said, "That's real nice, Dad, but there was a word for Crosby."

I braced myself. Dad cleared his throat and recited carefully, "You will see with your own eyes what God can do. You will walk to places that you can't imagine and say the words that God will teach you. The arm of the Lord will be with you, and you shall stomp on the works of the devil."

I had braced myself for this? I said to Dad, "That's all? I already know I can see and walk and say words. And I already have a plan for my life."

That last comment might have been one statement too many on my part. There was such a thing as doing God's will, but I wanted to write, and so far I had kept that plan secret from everybody. What if I found out that God didn't want me to write? What was I supposed to do about that?

Everyone was staring at me now, and I knew I had to say something. So I repeated cleverly, "That's all?" I was looking right at Dad Upland.

But it was Mom who answered me. "How much do you need, Crosby?"

I swung my gaze over to Mom. "You're the one who's told me all my life that God loves me and has a wonderful plan for my life. And you've told me hundreds of times that God told you to name me Crosby," I said earnestly and firmly. "So now I want to know why?"

"Yes, He did tell me that." Mom paused and then said quietly, "I think God has a way of getting his hook in us, so that we have pressing questions that make us desperate for answers. And then we keep on living and asking Him for more information."

"You mean you named me Crosby so I would ask God about it?" I asked in astonishment.

"Something like that," Mom said. "Mostly I liked the sound of it, and you have to admit, Bing Crosby does have a very sweet voice."

Now my mind jumped. "But how about hell?"

Dad Upland answered, "You never know what goes through someone's mind at the last second before death takes them. Always remember: the thief on the cross next to our Savior got it right with God just before he died. I've personally heard many people call out to God with their last breath in true repentance and ask for salvation."

Whatever tricks I had been using up to this point had now been demolished. Nothing had stopped the flow of information. I felt like someone had kicked me in the head.

I looked at Mom, and then something which had happened this morning suddenly clicked in my mind.

"You've read all the books in my cabinet, haven't you?" I said with full knowledge that it was so.

Mom nodded. "You have a wonderful collection, Crosby, though the cabinet you have it in is sometimes difficult to open. And those *Reader's Digest Condensed Books* are just not enough for me. Occasionally I need something that's a little more gritty and lifelike. I especially enjoyed the adventures of Ari Ben Canaan."

My mouth dropped open. "You've known all along?" I asked grimly.

"It's like Aunt Zonell says: the newspaper reports really horrible stories every day, but in books, at least you can enjoy some good writing. In fact, I've never told you, but when I was a young girl, I wanted to be a writer."

I gasped out loud and stared at my Mom. "That's what I want to be," I said weakly.

"Then what's stopping you?" Mom said emphatically.

"But I'm only a kid, and I don't know how to write stories," I said, a note of pleading and desperation in my voice.

"I think it takes time and study to learn. Nobody is a born writer. Why, with all the great books you have read, you're at least pointed in the right direction. Just keep at it and never give up."

Mom suddenly looked at everyone around the table. She stood up and said to Grandma, "Let's warm these plates up so we can enjoy this good food."

"I'm not hungry anymore," I said gloomily.

Grandma and Mom looked at each other and chuckled. "Oh, I think once we warm the food up, your appetite will return," Mom said.

The Mastons and Dad Upland began to hand their plates over to them, and I was forgotten for the moment.

I was feeling like, one way or another, some major issues in my life had been resolved, but at what cost? The changes had come, lurching and halting, to confront and embrace my skinny body and soul. Even though it was actually only a few days ago, it seemed like years had passed since I had made a very personal resolution not to cry in class anymore. That one change had turned out to be formidable and all-engulfing. One thing had led to another.

For one thing, my experiment in not crying in class had led to other experiments: like facing a few facts about my father and discarding my crutches and achieving some degree of reconciliation with Clyde Winston and recognizing how much I liked everything about Maria and ironing out a few wrinkles about my future as a writer.

It all seemed a little ironic to me. I wasn't the center as it turned out. I had received no guarantees. I thought change for the good would naturally give me a feeling of relief and peace and spine-tingling joy. Instead, what I had now was a lot of new information to sort out. I supposed the happy feelings would follow later. My choice now was to take care of business.

So while our plates were being warmed, I sat at our kitchen table, my mind leaping and sputtering and fizzling around, searching for a comparison or a parallel or perhaps even a raggedy figure of speech.

On the one hand, I'd been rolled through one of life's wringers, and now me and my thoughts were hung out to drip dry. All that information, coming in dribs and drabs and smacking me around had upset all the apples in my cart. I was hoping and praying I'd never have another such week in my life.

But on the other hand, if I concentrated really hard about it all, I concluded that I hadn't been told anything that I didn't already know in one form or another. After all, my message, gleaned from my reading, was the peopleness of people, and it meant that there was always hope. Big, beautiful, expectation of good hope. So I began to shrug off the gloom and practice what I preached: look to the future with hope.

I still loved my books, and I couldn't help but care about the characters in them. I wanted them to have better lives, but I was always captivated by their problems. I still worried about the Joad family being separated from Tom, and what about dear Rose and Sharon losing her baby? And Francie and Neeley Nolan suffered through poverty, and the tragic early death of their alcoholic father. I thought about my hero, Dov Landau, making his way through the stench-filled sewers of the Warsaw Ghetto so he could help the Jews who were being held captive and kept separated from the rest of the city's population behind the wall. And he survived Auschwitz and finally ended up doing pioneer work in Israel.

One by one our plates were warmed up in the oven and then set before us again. And Mom was right: once the food was reheated, our appetites instantly returned.

Sister Maston looked at me and said, "Crosby, you have heard so much about your life tonight. So what do you think? What do you plan to do now?"

"I see two things I need to concentrate on," I said expansively. "There is a variety store in Monte Vista across the street from Refredi's Market. It's owned and run by a couple named Abraham and Yetta Greenberg, and I've been trying to make friends with them for years. But I need to be more sensitive and kind if I expect them to talk to me about their lives. It's a real challenge, but I think I'm making progress. I've got a lot to learn from them."

I paused and then said quite openly, "And the second thing I need to do is to start writing if I want to be a writer, which means I need to be more broad-minded about people and not so narrow in my view. Like tonight: I could have missed out on remembering Velma's kindly wrinkled old face and just thought of her as a vile woman, but that's not what I think now. I have to unlearn a few things I've got in my head."

And now since it was Sister Maston I was talking to, I said, "I didn't tell you yet, but your brother is coming over this week to fix my Mom's vacuum cleaner, and maybe I could tell him about a great book to read when he's here."

In the end, I did loan Clyde Winston a book to read. He told me later that he wished he had been around in 1947 so he could have sailed from Peru all the way across the Pacific Ocean to Tahiti on a raft built out of balsa wood trees. He said he'd like to try catching sharks by the tail and pulling them on board the raft like the crew had done.

I wasn't trying to show off, but I told him that the raft had sailed 4,300 nautical miles in 101 days, and he looked offended and asked me indignantly, "Who doesn't know that?" And I told him, "Don't be so huffy. Friends don't talk to friends like that." And then he demanded, "Have you got any other books like that to read?" So I told him to take a look in the cabinet, and he did and offered to fix the hinges.

I'm looking forward to this Monday. I'm going to sit next to Maria at lunch and tell her that I admire her father and that I'm glad he knows my Uncle Hamlin. I'm going to tell her she's the prettiest girl in the school, and then I'm going to remind her that for an entire week I'd kept my promise: I hadn't cried once. And since school is almost out, I think I'm going to ask Mr. Lopez for a job this summer. Then I'll be able to contribute toward our rent payment, but also I'll have enough money left over so I can buy all the paperback books I want off the revolving rack at Abraham and Yetta's Variety Store and

Barber Shop. In addition, I'm going to buy a notebook so I can start writing my story down.

And after giving the two candidates some further analysis, I've decided that I was right all along: Mrs. Kennedy is the prettiest wife. So I'm going to suggest to Mom and Grandma that a vote for John Kennedy would be the right thing to do. This is going to be an interesting summer.

-THE END-

About the Author

Born in Palo Alto, California, John Edwards now lives and works in Upstate New York, where he has applied his hand over the years to teaching students of all ages—kindergarten through high school seniors—in a career spanning nearly forty years.

Widows and Orphans is the first novel in a trilogy about the life and times of protagonist, Crosby Hoggard. Later stories will find Crosby involved in the war in Vietnam.

John Edwards himself served with the Twenty-Fifth Infantry Division in Vietnam for a one-year tour of duty. Says Edwards, "One moment I was a student at West Valley College in Saratoga, California and the next moment I found myself making an Eagle Jump into War Zone C, near the Cambodian border."

Mr. Edwards currently resides in the Albany, New York, area with his wife, Deborah, and their son, John.